EMBER SHADOWS

and the FATES of

MOUNT NEVER

REBECCA KING

EMBER SHADOWS

and the FATES of MOUNT NEVER

Orion

ORION CHILDREN'S BOOKS

First published in Great Britain in 2022
by Hodder & Stoughton

1 3 5 7 9 10 8 6 4 2

Text copyright © Rebecca King, 2022
Illustrations copyright © Raquel Ochoa, 2022

The moral rights of the author and illustrator have been asserted.

A CIP catalogue record for this book
is available from the British Library.

ISBN 978 1 51010 995 7

Typeset in Sabon by Jouve (UK), Milton Keynes
Printed and bound in Great Britain by Clays Ltd, Elcograf S.p.A.

The paper and board used in this book are made
from wood from responsible sources.

Orion Children's Books
An imprint of
Hachette Children's Group
Part of Hodder & Stoughton Limited
Carmelite House
50 Victoria Embankment
London EC4Y 0DZ

An Hachette UK Company

www.hachette.co.uk
www.hachettechildrens.co.uk

To Luke, for all the adventures

1

Legs hanging over the side of the treehouse, the girl held a match to a white piece of card. The flame licked at its corner, but it wouldn't catch. Why wouldn't it just burn already? This was the only idea she had left. If she couldn't tear it apart, couldn't throw it away, couldn't burn it to ash – what else was there?

Ember blew out the flame and added the match to the pile of burnt sticks beside her. It was useless. She

turned back to the card. *Ember Shadows*. Just the sight of her name typed in black across the top was enough to make her queasy.

She stared out over Everspring. This was usually her favourite place to come for ideas. There was something about the thatched roofs of the village roundhouses, the way they huddled together like bees in a hive, and the way the people snaked between them; she liked to imagine that was how ideas moved in her brain, whizzing around, ready to be found.

It was best to climb up to the treehouse in the morning before anyone was awake, then she could see the sun rise over the treetops on the other side of the village, and people emerge from their houses one by one. But now, after a whole day of trying to get rid of her card, the sun had travelled right across the sky and was almost ready to disappear behind her.

In the orange glow, something caught Ember's eye. From the peak of Mount Never, towering over the village, three all-too-familiar shapes had begun their descent.

Surely there weren't more already? It had only been four days since her own had arrived. But she could make them out perfectly clearly: three rectangles floating down from the top of the mountain towards the village. They parted as they reached the roofs below, each white card taking a different path, until, one by one, they reached their destinations.

Ember watched one of the cards as it drifted downwards, slowly yet purposefully, until it landed squarely in the middle of a doormat. Ember had seen this sort of delivery enough times to know the cards were never swept away again, no matter how strong the wind. Instead, they would lie motionless, as if held down by some invisible force, waiting to be claimed.

She gave her card another glare and then turned away from the village. Dad had always said, *If you can't fix one problem, find another to work on.* So she stood and began hunting around for something to fix.

Last week, she had been working on the treehouse itself. A huge, four-day downpour had rotted part of the ladder and rusted the special hinges she had designed. Repairing those had been the priority, otherwise she wouldn't have been able to pull the ladder in after her and anyone could have climbed up. Juniper had offered to help, but the treehouse was the one thing that was truly Ember's. After all, she had built it herself nearly two years ago.

With inventions or inventions-in-progress covering almost every surface of the treehouse – spread across the shelves, the worktable in the centre and even hanging from the tree's branches above her – there was plenty to work on. But as she looked around, Ember couldn't find a problem worth fixing. They all seemed so insignificant since the arrival of her card. Half-heartedly, she picked up the bookrest she had been making for Juniper.

Finding the pieces for this one had involved a late-night salvaging mission to the kitchen. Mum had already asked about the missing cutlery, but she hadn't noticed the bottom hinge on the cupboard under the sink had disappeared yet. Lying about the missing forks and teaspoons had seemed like such a big deal at the time. Now Ember *wished* a missing piece of cutlery was her biggest problem.

Ember examined the half-made bookrest. She had managed to bend two forks into arms to hold the back of the book, and she had attached two teaspoon heads to the corners to keep the pages down. But one side wasn't quite right, not yet. She fiddled with the bolts.

Then she pulled off the teaspoon head. As she worked, an uneasiness began to take hold of her.

It started in her stomach, a feeling like a screw turning in the wrong-sized hole, and then it spread over her body and up her neck. Ember knew that jarring sensation too well; she had felt it before.

It was the feeling of being watched.

Her head snapped up and she frantically scanned the trees around her.

Nothing. Only the branches dancing in the breeze.

She must have been imagining it.

But as Ember peered nervously into the growing darkness, she couldn't stop her gaze from being pulled north, towards the source of all her problems.

Mount Never.

Over the years, Ember had spent hours staring up at that mountain and wondering how the rest of her life would unfold. Villagers always said that fate had big things planned for her, and she had drunk in every word of it, desperate for the day when she would finally know for sure.

Now she hated that mountain. Hated the way it sparkled in the sunset as though it might suddenly erupt into a kaleidoscope of rays, like light through a diamond. She hated its layers mottled together at the seams, each colour blending into the next. Dark green at the base, turning to orange, then violet, deep red, then gold. At the top, right at the very summit of the mountain, it became a black so dark it seemed as though a curtain of night had been wrapped around the peak. But most of all she hated the long wooden building balancing on the very top. No one believed her of course, but Ember knew she had seen it move in the wind, teetering on the edge as though one day it might fall and slide right down the mountain like one of its stupid cards.

Still, the magic of Mount Never fascinated her. It was captivating, mysterious, the way it delivered everyone their destiny, each one printed on a Fate Card and sent down from its peak. There was no telling when a person's card might come; the council had never managed to figure out the puzzling pattern of their arrival. So far, none had come after a person's twelfth birthday, but there had been some that came so early the child was barely able to read it themselves. Of course, siblings' cards usually arrived close together.

The elders of the village thought this was probably because the fates of family members were so closely intertwined. Ember's stomach clenched at the thought. That meant Juniper's would be any day now.

There had been moments – before her card had arrived – when Ember had been sure it would spell out her every dream and confirm her fate as an inventor. Other days, she was haunted by stories of cards that had come before. There were whispered tales of a girl whose card had come when Ember was a baby. Her fate had been so criminal that the council was forced to send her beyond Border River where she lived off stolen food, broke into homes at night, and spent her days as a nomad, fulfilling her destiny, exactly as the mountain had predicted. The thought would gnaw away at Ember, that maybe her card would deal her something equally as lonely and terrible.

The idea that it would come completely blank had never even wormed its way into her tangle of thoughts.

But here it was.

She had to get rid of it. It had to be done quickly or everyone would find out about her empty fate, and then—

No. She didn't need to think about that. She was going to get rid of her Fate Card tomorrow, she had to.

Windows in the village began to light up like stars as the sun's glow faded, sending Mount Never into darkness.

It was time to go home.

2

Ember could feel the village humming with news as she wove between houses, avoiding the path so she wouldn't run into anyone on the way home. The three Fate Cards she had seen falling from the mountain meant three destinies revealed, and there wasn't a single person in Everspring who wouldn't be talking about them. People would be asking if she had received hers soon enough.

Finally, she reached the red brick of her family roundhouse, nestled among autumn leaves on the edge of the forest, and raced forward.

As soon as Ember opened the front door, the warmth of her home wrapped itself around her and Juniper appeared in the hallway, rushing forward for her own embrace. As usual, Juniper must have been listening for Ember's return, waiting to update her on the latest news.

'Three cards came!' her sister squealed, before Ember had even had time to pull off her coat. 'One of them was Summer's! She's going to make boats. Isn't that great?'

Ember and Juniper knew Summer from school.

'Didn't she want—'

'To be a baker?' Juniper was the only person who knew Ember well enough to finish her sentences. 'She *thought* she wanted to be a baker, but she was totally wrong and now she's going to be working in the dock with her dad.'

Despite the excitement in Juniper's voice, Ember noticed that her eyes were worried and she was nervously fiddling with the loose strands of hair that had fallen out of her plait.

'What is it?' said Ember. She pulled Juniper towards her and undid the plait fully, then began neatly re-plaiting it, weaving her sister's blonde hair together into a long braid as she did most mornings.

'Nothing.' Juniper paused. 'Just . . . yours will be here soon, won't it?'

Ember tied off the plait and wrapped her arm around Juniper's shoulder. Together, they looked up at the family's Fate Cards. They had been collected together, framed and hung proudly by the entrance.

Each of the nine cards was unique, the owner's entire destiny crammed into a space no bigger than Ember's shoe. Words had been typed tightly together to squeeze in as much detail as possible – some horizontal, some vertical, but every inch filled with facts about the life they would lead, where they would live, who they would marry, what they would be. Aunt Genevieve had been fated a life so full, the ink had even carried over to the back of the card. And of course, in the middle of each card, there was always the number, showing how many years they would live.

'What was Summer's number?' Ember asked.

'Seventy-eight,' said Juniper. 'That seems like a good age to die, right?'

Ember nodded. It was a strange question. *No* age was a good age to die. But given that some of the cards came down from the mountain with a number that didn't even reach adulthood, seventy-eight seemed like a very good age to go.

Between the cards, their great-grandfather had painted a tree, so that each Fate Card looked as though it hung from a branch, their fates intertwined together as generations passed. Every spot on the tree had been taken except for three, where blank spaces lay waiting; one for Juniper, one for Ember, and one where their father's missing card should have been.

'Only ours left now,' said Juniper, her usual sing-song voice low and faint.

'It will be all right,' said Ember, and squeezed her shoulder. 'Your card is going to be great. You've got nothing to worry about.'

But Juniper simply nodded, still staring at the frame. 'I wish it was here already. Or yours was. It's horrible waiting all the time, not knowing anything.'

Ember loved her little sister more than anyone else in the world, but she couldn't tell her about the blank card. She just couldn't. Juniper was worried enough about her own card; telling her would only make things worse. Thankfully, like everyone else, it seemed she didn't suspect a thing. No one knew the card had arrived already.

Ember swallowed down the truth and plastered a smile on her face.

'Look, I know it's hard waiting, but you're right. Mine will be here before my birthday next week, and then yours will come. Or maybe it will even beat mine here, and you'll be the winner.'

Juniper's head whizzed round, her competitive streak switched on. 'What do I win?'

'Well, how about you can have four books from my bookshelf?'

Juniper's eyes widened and she nodded slowly, as if weighing up the offer. '*Any* four? Even the ones on the top shelf? Your favourites?'

'Any.' Ember crouched down, putting a hand under Juniper's chin. 'And you know, we can work it out together, whatever your card says. Even if it says you're going to be the toilet cleaner for the village, or a brown leaf collector, or a hermit who lives in a hole underground.'

Juniper let out a giggle and grabbed Ember's hand, squeezing her fingers until they hurt. 'You're right. And I can't wait to see what your card says. Your destiny is going to be amazing, I know it is. I think you'll be a Council Leader.'

Ember could almost feel the empty card in her bag screaming to get out, to jump inside the frame and reveal that, actually, fate had absolutely nothing in store for her whatsoever.

'What's Mum making for tea?' asked Ember, trying to change the subject. But Juniper just shrugged, her plait bouncing around her shoulders as she faced the frame once again, this time with a stern gaze, as if willing her card to arrive first.

They didn't look like sisters, not really. Ember was tall for her age and Juniper was tiny, even for an eight-year-old. There was no trace in Juniper's hair of the auburn colour that burnt Ember's own. Juniper had baby blue eyes with flecks of grey and light skin, while Ember's eyes were green, her skin browner. Only the matching freckles across the noses gave them away. Maybe that was why Ember liked them so much.

'Want a surprise?' said Ember. 'I'm working on an invention for you.' She reached round to her backpack to pull out the bookrest. 'I think you'll like it. It's going to be called the Book Cutler, like cuddler and cutlery all mixed together. When you're reading—'

'I wish I knew what Dad's card had said.' It was the smallest whisper, but it halted Ember's train of thought, the way it did whenever Juniper brought him up.

Ember opened her mouth, but what was there to say? They both knew what had happened to their father. No one knew why his card had disappeared, but there was nothing Ember could do to change what had happened, no matter how much she wished otherwise.

'Actually I think your present is in my room,' she said, shouldering her backpack again and pretending she hadn't heard Juniper's words. 'I'll give it to you later.' Leaving Juniper, she followed the corridor round the house to her bedroom.

The village roundhouses had been designed by her grandmother long ago, and to Ember they were the most ingenious design. Each one was a perfect circle, complete with a ring around the edge making a hallway to access all the rooms. The inner circle was split in half. One of the halves was split again to hold the kitchen and living room, where she and Juniper read together on rainy days, and the other half held three small bedrooms and a bathroom. Everything about its layout felt safe, as though nothing could hurt their family when it was inside that circle, the hallway a protective embrace around their home, keeping them together.

Ember's room was as disorganised as her treehouse, which was exactly how she liked it. Above the bed frame, which was carved to fit the curved wall, she had hung shelves to store piles of inventions, some finished, some still in progress, some no more than ideas that hadn't made it to the treehouse yet.

Then there were the lights. That was the one problem with the shape of their home: having the hallway on the outside meant the only light came from

small panes of glass built into the roof. To brighten things up, Ember had collected strings of lights to hang from the walls and ceiling, and, when they were all turned on, each one hung like a firefly over her head.

Flicking them on now, Ember closed the door behind her and sank on to her bed, trying to shake the guilt she felt whenever Juniper brought up their father. She had enough to think about at the moment.

She opened her bag and, slowly, as if it were made of something toxic, Ember pulled out her card.

The white space glared back at her and she slid it under the pillow, heart thumping.

No one's card had ever come empty before. Never. No matter how bad their fate was, they had always been given *something*. She had wasted the whole day thinking up ideas to get rid of it that hadn't worked and now there were only four days until her twelfth birthday. Cards always arrived before then. If she kept it a secret much longer, people would start to become suspicious.

Soon, she might have to come clean.

Soon, but not yet.

'Are you all right in here?'

She sat bolt upright, spinning round to look at the door where Mum stood, leaning against the frame.

'Sorry, you scared me. Didn't hear you.' A tiny corner of the card was still poking out from under her pillow. Her skin prickled.

Mum walked over to the bed, ducking below a particularly low bulb, and sat down, pulling Ember's feet on to her lap. 'No Fate Card again today?'

Ember shook her head and shuffled up the bed towards the pillow to cover the card, before meeting her mum's gaze. Her mum had always been beautiful, with long, chocolate brown hair that curled over her shoulders and perfectly framed her angular face and dark eyes. There were definitely traces of Juniper in her smile and the way she looked when she was thinking something through, but there wasn't much of Ember that she could see reflected in her mum.

'You'll get it soon. And you know, whatever is on that card, we love you regardless. Dad did too.'

Since Dad had died, it was much harder to predict her mum's mood. Some days she was the strongest, most independent woman. Other days she was impossible to talk to, as fragile as a daisy in a thunderstorm.

Thankfully, today seemed like one of the better days.

'You know,' Mum continued, 'Juniper told me she thinks you'll be a Council Leader. Imagine that, my Ember leading the village!'

'She said that to me, too,' said Ember. 'But, you know, I might not be anything important. I might have—' She tried words out in her mind but couldn't find anything that fit. *Nothing? An empty future?* How could she know what the blank card meant?

'Every job is something, Ember. Everyone has value.'

'I know. It has to be something good though, because otherwise Dad died and it was all—'

'No,' Mum said, grabbing Ember's hand. 'What happened to Dad doesn't have anything to do with what's on your card. You don't owe him, or the rest of the family, anything.'

Mum wouldn't say that if she saw what was under my pillow, Ember thought.

'Sometimes what's on the card surprises us. But that doesn't mean it's not right.' Mum tucked her hair behind her left ear, and a dandelion earring that Ember had made her sparkled under all the lights. 'It's not always easy to accept our fate, but it's our duty. Think about all of the jobs in the village. Everyone plays their part and, together, we're a community.'

The idea hung between them for a moment. Every person was a cog in the community's mechanics. Without a purpose, Ember would be nothing more than a spare part.

'Only your father knew this,' her mum went on, 'but before my card arrived, I wanted to be a writer. I had written nearly an entire book when I was little, an adventure story . . . but once I found out that books weren't on my card, I put it to one side.'

'How did you just . . . stop?'

'It was my fate, Ember,' her mum said simply.

'But Mum, what if someone didn't follow their card? What if—'

'Impossible. Fate is fate. It will always right itself. You might think you're choosing another path, but it will always lead back to your fate. You *know* that.'

'But what about Dad's card? What happened to it? And did it say that—'

'Ember!' her mum said sharply, cutting her off. She closed her eyes for a second and Ember watched her shoulders rise and fall as she calmed herself. 'Enough,' she said at last. 'What happened, has happened. The card has gone and we will never know for sure what it said. Anything I *think* it might have said . . . well, it's only a foggy, obscured memory.'

Mum stood up and pulled the drawer of the bedside table open to retrieve Ember's most prized possession. It was a collection of old tools kept in a silver case, tarnished at the corners, with a brown leather handle. Etched into the silver was a single line of script in her father's handwriting, which read, *Your only limit is your imagination.*

'Now, why don't you make me something exciting before we eat?' she said, smiling down at Ember. 'I need you to fix the kitchen cupboard door too, one of the hinges seems to have walked off.' She raised her eyebrows. 'Know anything about that?'

Ember managed to return a smile and sat up, taking the case from her mum. But once the door had closed, she pushed it straight back into the drawer. She didn't have time to make anything new. She had less than four days to figure out what to do about her empty Fate Card, before the whole village became suspicious.

Because if they found out she had no future, no destiny, and no part to play in the community . . .

Ember shuddered to think what might happen then.

3

The next day, once school was done, Ember followed the pebbled path out to Border River. Her feet crunched on the dry leaves as she went past the other houses, the vegetable patches and the pig farm.

She hadn't been sure whether or not she would actually have the courage to do this. But no matter how much the water terrified her, she needed to try. If this didn't work, she didn't know what she would do. She had nothing else.

Ember always thought of her village like a compass, with Mount Never looming over them from the north. Her school and her treehouse were at the west side of the village and from there the main path stretched into the centre, past the houses and all the way out east to the forest, where Juniper spent most of her time watching the animals in the trees. Juniper seemed to blend in amongst the forest, and the animals were more at ease with her than anyone in the village. To the south was Ember's least favourite place of all – Border River, which flowed along the boundary of her town to the villages beyond.

Everyone else had rushed home after school, trying to get inside before the wind picked up, so thankfully no one else seemed to be out. It suddenly struck Ember that she might only have a few days left of school now. Maybe they would let her stay. But how would they even decide what to do with her without a Fate Card showing her path? Only last week a boy had been moved from Pre-Card to Post-Card school, where he was specialising in bookbinding. One girl had been put into engineering and science class after she got her card. But without a card telling them what Ember needed to learn for her future, how would they know what to teach her?

She pulled the zip higher on her winter jacket and hunched her shoulders. The air was getting colder each day now and the winds were gathering in the trees and tumbling into the valley as they did every year before winter hit. Ember much preferred the beginning of autumn, when the trees began to shed their leaves like skin, and she'd sit in the forest with

Juniper, inventing while her sister searched for animal homes. Or they'd spend the weekends designing treasure hunts, and Ember would pretend her sister's clues were challenging, even if she could see the prize before they had started.

It was strange to think she had lived a whole four years before Juniper came along. Ember didn't have a single memory from before her sister was by her side. She just hoped this would work. Keeping a secret from Juniper felt wrong.

Finally, Ember passed the Council Hut, reached the edge of the path and arrived at Border River. Only a handful of people were allowed on to the water nowadays, mostly council members, who travelled to neighbouring towns for news and trade. The rest were people destined for a life beyond Everspring, or people whose cards said they would commit terrible crimes and were sent away.

Ember tried to focus on the path and forget about the rumbling current. She tried not to think of her dad, and that day in the water that had changed everything. But even from the corner of her eye she could see the waves leaping up, thumping into the riverbank and curling in on themselves as the water rushed through the wide channel. Careful not to get too close to the edge, she sat down against a rock and unzipped her bag.

The blank card stared up at her. Burning, tearing, cutting – none of that had destroyed it, but this, this would. It *must*. And then, once she had got rid of it, surely another card would fall from the mountain, one that actually contained a fate.

One hand on the rock to keep herself steady, Ember crouched and leant towards the edge of the riverbank. The water thundered past her, dragging branches, leaves and other fragments from the forest down into its depths. The wide channel stretched out ahead, the opposite riverbank at least a fallen tree's distance from her.

She clutched the card, took one final look at it and flung it into the water. *Good riddance.*

It spun from her hand, pirouetted in the air, down, down towards the water; but before it hit the surface, the wind caught it, bounced it up away from the river, and the card sailed back through the air, landing at her feet.

'No, no, no,' she said. 'I don't want you! I want a different one!'

She threw it again, launching it as far as she could downstream, straight into the waves. For a second, she thought the water had swallowed it, but the river only chewed it for a moment, then coughed it out and, like a boomerang, the card flitted back to her.

Again and again she tried, and again and again the card calmly floated back to her. She gripped the sides of it, tugging at it and twisting, but it held its shape like steel. It wouldn't break.

No matter what she tried, she was stuck with an empty fate. Dad would be so disappointed.

Exhausted, Ember sank down against the rock and, as she did, she heard something rustle behind her. She froze.

A moment later she felt the pressure of a pair of eyes. Something was watching her.

Her heart beating loudly inside her chest, Ember looked around. There, as she had dreaded, was an origami bird.

The folded paper creature clung to a tree branch metres away from her on the edge of the riverbank. From its perch, it stared down at Ember, two beady eyes watching her every move.

Her hands grew damp and her fingers began to tingle as she clutched her Fate Card. She had seen the bird before, or others like it at least. The first time had been the day of the accident, the day Dad died. Since then they had appeared whenever she was alone, watching, waiting, staring at her with their strange mirror-like eyes, blinking out from their featherless faces.

The omens.

She knew they were omens, everyone did. The crow-like bodies of these mythical birds weren't innocent like the paper cranes or swans children folded. While their white bodies were paper and smooth, their eyes were like those of live birds, blinking, moving, and black as a shadow. They seemed to narrow and stare at her as a person's might.

Once, in her treehouse, one of the birds had caught a spider. She had watched in horror as the animal's long folded beak had opened and pulled the legs from the poor creature. Then the bird had hopped over the spider and watched as it panicked and slowly died.

There was something terrible about them. If the villagers knew she had been seeing them for years, that they had been following her—

'Ember?' called a voice.

The bird's eyes flicked from Ember to the voice's owner, before it burst into flames. Bright sparks hovered in the air for half a breath, and it was gone.

It disappeared so quickly, as all the birds had done when anyone else approached. While Ember was grateful no one else had spotted her with the omens yet, her mind couldn't help whispering that there must be something wrong with her. Either they were warning her of something, something only she could know, or she had imagined them each and every time. Which was worse, she wasn't sure.

'I've been looking for you.'

The voice dragged her back to reality. It was Wisteria Daylands, the Council Leader. Her distinctive long ruby-red cloak hung around her shoulders.

The Fate Card. It was still in her hands.

Ember stuffed it back in her bag as she stood up. Hopefully Ms Daylands' eyesight wasn't good enough to have spotted the small white shape.

'Ms Daylands, hi!'

'Do you mind if I sit?' Ms Daylands said, gesturing at the rock Ember had been leaning against. Ember nodded as Ms Daylands perched on it, but not before brushing off some imaginary dust. Over her shoulder, Ember scanned the tree for the bird, for any trace of its existence. But there was nothing.

'Your mother tells me your card hasn't arrived yet,' said Ms Daylands.

This was it, Ember thought. She was going to be found out. She knew it.

'You know,' Ms Daylands went on, not waiting for a response. 'A hundred years ago, people didn't get Fate Cards. They didn't know anything about what their future held. Can you imagine how terrifying that must have been?'

Ember said nothing. She knew exactly how terrifying that was.

Ms Daylands pushed her tight grey curls off her face, her lips turning up into a smile as she watched the river. 'But then the cards began to come, and people knew what would happen in their lives. There was no need for panic any more.' She looked at Ember. 'Still, sometimes people don't like what their card says.'

'What can they do then?' said Ember, maybe a little too quickly.

'Well, that's the thing, my dear. Nothing. Imagine if we didn't have these cards. Fate is still fate, destiny must still be fulfilled. I would still be Council Leader even without my card. Our lives would continue in the same way. The only difference is in the knowing.' She gestured as she talked, her brown arms thin and wrinkled, as though she might be able to illustrate it all for Ember in the air.

Ember nodded and the pit in her stomach started to grow. She was definitely about to get found out.

'Fate doesn't change, my dear,' Ms Daylands said. 'There are villages beyond Everspring, with skies as blue as ours and trees as tall as ours. Some of them also have the gift of the cards, but most of them are not so lucky. Even so, fate is the same everywhere. Do you understand what I'm saying?'

'I think so,' Ember said. 'Just because some people don't know their fate, it doesn't mean it can change.'

There was a long silence. Did Ms Daylands know about her card? If not, why was she telling her this? 'I think I need to get home.' Ember said finally, pulling her bag on to her back.

'I think that might be a good idea,' Ms Daylands said.

Ember swallowed, turned back to the path and then stopped. 'Ms Daylands, why are you telling me all of this?'

Ms Daylands sighed and looked out over the river, before slowly turning back to Ember. 'Your sister's card arrived today,' she said. 'Promise me that you will remember what we discussed when you learn what fate has in store for her.'

4

Juniper.

She had to get home.

Ember sprinted back up the path without another word to Ms Daylands, not slowing until she swung around the final corner before her house, skidded on the path and rebalanced, right outside the front door.

The lights were on.

For a second, Ember couldn't move. Juniper and her mum would be on the other side of the door. What did Ms Daylands' warning mean? Ember's stomach tightened as slowly, she reached out, grabbed the latch on the door, and pushed.

Something was wrong.

The house was quiet.

She stepped forward. She saw that Juniper's card was still missing from the family frame; clearly she was in no rush to display it. She started around the corridor, past the kitchen, past her own bedroom, and towards Juniper's.

'Juniper?' she called out. 'Mum?'

Then she heard it.

It was soft at first, muffled, like someone had turned the volume down on the world. But as she got closer to Juniper's room, Ember was able to make out what it was: the sound of crying.

Uneasily, she pushed open Juniper's door to find her tangled in a mangled mess of bedsheets.

'Go away!' Juniper's head was buried in a pillow, her voice faint though her body shook violently with every sob.

'What's wrong, what happened?' Ember asked, dreading the answer. But Juniper went on crying. Could it be that *both* their fates were blank?

Ember looked around, searching for the card. Usually perfectly pristine, today the room was a mess. Juniper's dressing table had been swept clean, brushes on the floor and a mirror smashed into pieces. Her paintings of forest animals were in tatters. Sketches of dragonflutters, froghoppers and treebears had been pulled from the walls and littered around the room. It looked as though a wild animal had broken in and destroyed every part of Juniper's life.

And there, in the very middle of the room, was the culprit. A white card lying on the floor. Even from this distance, Ember could see it was packed with words. So it wasn't blank. Then why was Juniper crying?

Ember stood up and walked towards the card as though it might bite. She reached her hand out, and then she saw it.

Beneath her sister's name, woven into a patchwork of words and phrases that barely reached the edges of the card, a single digit glared back at her.

8

No.

8

'No,' she whispered. 'Juniper—'

'That's right.' Juniper's body rose from her bedsheets but it was someone else's face that stared back, red eyes bloodshot, skin puffy, and hair sticking out at the sides. The tears had stopped and now there was nothing but anger carved into her features. 'I'm an *eight*. I'm going to die before my next birthday. You can keep your stupid bet and your books – I won't need them.'

She spat the words out and Ember stepped back. Another step. Maybe if she kept stepping backwards she might be able to rewind the last minute and play it out differently.

'You told me I had nothing to worry about,' Juniper said, the sobs threatening to overtake her again. 'You said it would be all right. But I don't even have a year left! I could have a week, or maybe a day. I don't even know.' She sank back down, and started sobbing into the pillow again.

'It's got to be wrong, it has to be,' Ember said, picking the card up. 'There must be some mistake.'

Juniper couldn't be meant to die. Ember blinked,

screwing her eyes closed tight, as if when she opened them the eight would have changed to something less terrible. It had to be a dream. This couldn't be real. It wasn't real.

But the eight stared back at her, gleaming against the white background. The words around it were meaningless – family, school, treehouse, parties. It was all nonsense to fill the rest of her short life.

'Juniper, where's Mum?'

'I told her I wanted to be on my own.' Juniper gathered her breath and sat up. The anger had faded but the tears kept rolling silently. 'I think she's sleeping.'

Ember rushed over to her bed and wrapped an arm around Juniper's shoulders, pulling her close. There was no way their mum would be sleeping. She would be distraught. But Ember wasn't going to worry her sister about that now.

'What am I going to do, Ember?' Juniper whispered.

It was the impossible question. After days of trying to destroy her own card, Ember knew there was nothing they could do. This was what Ms Daylands had been trying to say: that whether they knew about it or not, Juniper was always going to die young. Having the card just meant they knew how little time she had left.

Ember tried to grasp the idea, but it kept escaping like smoke in her hands. It didn't make sense. All that time growing up together, chasing each other, their games in the forest, their secrets, their memories – it was all going to end. And it could happen at any moment. Juniper's ninth birthday was only eight months away.

The rest of her life without Juniper, without her little sister. She couldn't imagine it. The worries about her own blank fate had disappeared, leaving only the terror of Juniper's fate in its place.

She had to do something.

'Do you remember when we were tiny,' she said at last. 'We used to go out into the forest and I would climb those really tall trees? You'd get so worried. You thought I would fall.'

Juniper's head bobbed against her shoulder.

'I told you then that I could do anything, didn't I?' Ember continued.

'You told me you could fly.'

Ember smiled. 'That's right. Well, I have to tell you a secret.'

Juniper pulled away, looking up at her. Ember spotted a flicker of her sister again, the sister she knew. 'What is it?'

'You can't tell anyone. Not even Mum. But I wasn't lying. I really can do anything.'

She gripped Juniper's hand and held it close to her chest.

'So,' she carried on. 'You need to stop crying and leave all of this to me. Because I can fix it.'

Juniper pulled her hand back. 'Thanks, Ember, but I'm not a baby any more. I know that's not true.' She untangled her body and turned away, saying softly, 'If you could do anything, Dad wouldn't have died.'

The air ripped from Ember's lungs and she lurched forward. It was as if she had been punched in the stomach.

Juniper lay down, pulled the bedsheets up around her chin, and rolled over. It was clear she wanted Ember to go.

Ember slowly got off the bed and walked to the door, but before leaving the room she paused. As much to her sister as herself, she whispered, 'I will fix this, Juniper. I promise.'

5

Two days later, Ember was staring up at the mountain from her treehouse. Cogs ticked in her mind as new ideas whirred around her head, only to be discarded. She was working on the bookrest for Juniper, trying to keep her hands busy as her mind worked, but it seemed so stupid now, such a pointless present. She gave up and stuffed it into her bag.

It had been impossible getting Juniper out of her room – not for school, not for food, not to put her card in the frame. She wouldn't move. Mum had refused to talk about it at all; her eyes glazed over whenever Ember tried to speak to her and a sour smell lingered on her clothes.

But outside the house, it was all anyone in Everspring seemed to be talking about. Ember couldn't remember a time she'd felt so visible – everyone spoke in hushed whispers as she walked to school, nudging each other and pointing at her, and then falling silent when she walked past.

It was the same in class. Ember's *best* friend had always been Juniper of course, but she'd found it easy enough to make other friends at school – everyone seemed to like her inventions and her games of make-believe. Now though, not a single person would even sit next to her. It was as if she were the wrong end of a magnet, repelling everyone within five metres.

The four hours of Mr Coal's class had washed over her today. Usually, she would have soaked in every word of his lessons on history, geography, astronomy, foreign mythology and botany, getting as much information from Pre-Card school so she was ready to progress to Post-Card learning. She'd been so sure she'd be put in the engineering class to learn more about the nuts and bolts of machines, how things worked, how to use all the ideas she had to make the village a better place.

None of it mattered now, of course.

'Ember?'

She sprang to her feet. Juniper was out of bed.

'Wait a second,' she called, looking through the gap in the floor to where her sister stood below. She pushed the ladder through and unfolded it, the hinges stretching flat as the ladder extended, piece by piece, down to Juniper.

Juniper climbed up and when she reached Ember, the pair of them pulled the ladder back up and folded it away. Then they sat down on the edge of the treehouse overlooking the village without speaking for a while.

Finally, Juniper broke the silence.

'I'm sorry for what I said about Dad,' she said. 'I didn't mean that it was your fault, I just meant, you can't fix this.'

'But I—'

'Ember, *no one* can fix this. It's fate.' She turned to Ember and smiled, her eyes still puffy from crying. 'Anyway, it's your birthday tomorrow, and I didn't want to miss your card arriving.'

Guilt twisted in Ember's stomach. The secret she'd been holding felt like it might burst from her at any moment. And like Juniper said, Ember's birthday was tomorrow. Everyone would know soon enough.

'I need to tell you something.'

Juniper frowned. 'What is it?'

Ember breathed in, and pulled her backpack towards her. She paused for a second, the weight of what she was about to show Juniper rolling over her like a wave, before she pulled out the card and handed it to her sister.

'I don't understand,' Juniper whispered. 'What is this?'

'It's my card.'

'But you haven't got—'

'It arrived about a week ago. It came here, to the treehouse, late at night. I didn't tell anyone because . . .' She gestured at the card. 'Because it's empty.'

Juniper turned it over, as if she were looking for words on the other side.

'But . . . what does it mean?'

Ember rubbed her cheek, itching the skin as she swallowed. 'I don't know. I've been trying to figure it out for ages. I thought maybe I could get a real fate if I got rid of this one, but I can't get rid of it. I've tried ripping it, burning it, everything.'

'Me too,' said Juniper. 'Nothing works.'

Ember was surprised. She didn't think her little sister would have dared.

'Has this ever happened before?' Juniper asked.

'I don't think so.'

Juniper pulled her knees tight to her chest and shivered as she stared at the card. Ember tried to ignore the niggling thought at the back of her mind, the small voice telling her that her sister already looked ill, her skin a bit grey, her cheeks slightly sunken and her shoulders slumped.

She took a deep breath, ready to tell Juniper about the strange, folded paper birds that only she saw, when Juniper spoke.

'Poor Mum,' she whispered.

She was right. With Juniper's card an eight, and Ember's empty, what would happen to their mum? When Dad had died, it had been hard for everyone, but Mum had dealt with it the worst. Ember remembered nights when she would disappear into her bedroom, emerging the following afternoon with headaches and dark circles around her eyes. Juniper's card was already too much for her to bear. What would happen when she learnt about Ember's?

She wouldn't tell them about the birds, Ember decided. A blank Fate Card was bad enough. Both Juniper and Mum had always believed in omens and bad luck; this might tip them over the edge.

'You'll have to tell her soon,' said Juniper gently. 'It's your birthday tomorrow.'

Ember nodded. 'I know. But first, I have to think of a plan.'

*

By the time Ember reached the Council Hut, the

sun had nearly set. She and Juniper had sat on the edge of the treehouse talking for hours. It felt good to share the secret about her card, like everything was out in the open between them – well, nearly everything.

But then, standing in front of the Council Hut, Ember spotted a folded paper bird, perched on the roof, waiting for her, and her uneasiness returned. It twisted its body to stare down at her.

'Leave me alone!' she muttered, trying to shoo it off, knowing it wouldn't work. It never did.

She didn't have time to worry about the birds now. Whether she was imagining them, or something was wrong with her, it didn't matter – she needed a plan to help Juniper and find herself a new Fate Card, and the Council Hut was the first step.

The circular building was the biggest in Everspring, a thatched-roof, one-room structure that everyone from the village could fit inside. It was used mostly for parties and important meetings to discuss community issues; although, because everything was already written on the cards, there wasn't much that was up for debate. Even so, Ms Daylands and the other six council members still called the village together every once in a while to keep things running smoothly and make sure everyone was clear about their fate.

Imagine the meeting they would have about my card, Ember thought. The idea made her smirk, just a bit.

Ember took a deep breath and knocked on the door, and the bird above her unfolded its wings, burst into a fizz of cinders, and disappeared.

The rustling of papers sounded from inside. When Ms Daylands opened the door, she didn't look at all surprised to see Ember.

'Come on in,' she said. She was wearing an emerald-green cloak today, and her curls were piled on top of her head. 'Is it just you? You didn't bring your sister?'

'She's not really up to it at the moment,' said Ember, as she followed Ms Daylands into the large room. Mum called it the Magnificent Room, and it did feel magnificent, with its thatched roof reaching high up into the sky, like a witch's hat from a storybook.

Ms Daylands led Ember across the circle towards her desk, which was covered in mountains of paper and files. The pair settled in two tall-backed chairs, either side of the chaotic surface.

Ms Daylands pushed her glasses up to the top of her nose and leant forward. 'Now, how can I help, my dear?'

Ember bit her lip. She may as well start with the most difficult question.

'I wanted to ask about my father's card. Did it say that he was going to die when he did? Because I was thinking, if it changed, then maybe Juniper's could—'

Ms Daylands held her hand up to cut Ember off and sighed. 'We've been over this before, Ember. Fates do not change. What happened with your father was tragic, but there was nothing anyone could have done to change it.'

'But . . . how do we *know* his fate didn't change? His card disappeared. And no one can remember what was on it, not even my mum.'

'I see no reason to believe anything other than your father fulfilled his fate, just as the rest of us will.' Ms Daylands smiled at her sympathetically. 'Look, I know how difficult the arrival of Juniper's card must be for you, Ember,' she said. 'But everything truly does happen for a reason, and so you must not fear the arrival of your own card. Did your mother tell you the story of the boy who feared the cards?'

Ember shook her head.

'Good,' said Ms Daylands. 'It's much too dangerous a story to tell children. So I'm trusting you now, Ember. You keep this between us.'

Ember nodded as Ms Daylands took a deep breath. 'It happened twenty-five years ago,' she began, 'when your parents were children waiting for their own cards. The village was as it is now, full of wonderful people carrying out their true purpose. But one day, a boy went missing.'

'Missing?' *People don't go missing in Everspring,* thought Ember.

'Precisely. He, too, was eleven years old, but he was terrified of what the future might hold, and so he ran away. We found an oar near the river and a note saying he had left for another village. But no matter how much we searched the river and all the villages both upstream and down, he was never found.'

Ember knew all too well what it felt like to be scared of what might be on your card.

'The point is,' Ms Daylands went on, 'you mustn't be afraid. You must find the strength to accept whatever fate Mount Never deals you.'

'But what if I don't want to accept it!' Ember said, suddenly angry at Ms Daylands' calm voice. 'Surely there's something we can do! There *must* be a way of changing things. Hasn't anyone ever gone up Mount Never to find out where the cards come from? Maybe if I could—'

'No.' Ms Daylands interrupted her firmly. 'It has never been in anyone's fate to climb the mountain. Anyway, my dear, you'd have to be mad to go up there. Just think about the stories of terrible omens, paper birds and realms full of wild magic.'

Ms Daylands leant closer still.

'And there is more,' she whispered. 'Anyone who steps foot on that mountain is tangling with something even more dangerous than magic and paper birds, so the legends say. You see, if you tangle with fate, you do the unthinkable. You wipe your future away.'

'Wipe it away?'

Ms Daylands nodded, her dark eyes wide. 'Your Fate Card becomes empty. The words disappear. There is nothing but the unknown for someone who steps foot on that mountain. A blank fate . . .' She shuddered. 'Well, you see now why it is so important to trust the cards. It might be difficult, but, my dear, that's just the way things are.'

Ember nodded calmly, but in her head, an idea was already sprinting around, bouncing from one side to the other, growing with every second. She *already* had a blank future.

There was nothing that the mountain could wipe away from her.

Ember knew she would get no more help from Ms Daylands. Pretending she had taken the advice to heart, Ember thanked Ms Daylands and quickly left the Council Hut.

As she walked home, a warm feeling began flickering in her chest. It was a familiar feeling, one that had disappeared recently, but now it was back. It started to grow, glowing and spreading through her chest. Dad used to call it a Fixer's Feeling, the sense that you could make something better. Back then, he'd told her that while it was sometimes easier to ignore the feeling, it was always best to try and use it – because, that way, you could improve the world.

She let her idea explode in her mind like a firework.

It was about time someone climbed Mount Never.

6

Finally, Ember had a plan.

By the time she got home, Juniper had gone to bed already, and Mum went not long after. Ember could hear their heavy breathing as they slept. Time to get to work.

She tucked her hair behind her ears and surveyed her room. It was hard deciding what to pack for a completely unknown journey, but there had to be a few things that would come in handy.

To the right of her bed was her wardrobe. She didn't take anything from it – she wouldn't be gone long enough to need a change of clothes, she hoped. The bookshelf offered nothing useful either; she couldn't exactly take a stack of her favourite novels with her.

She moved to her small desk where her favourite photograph stood, their last one as a whole family. The picture was a bit faded but she could still see herself on Dad's shoulders, and Juniper on Mum's. They had been for a picnic down by the river that day, like they'd done most weekends before Dad died. She slid it into her bag and examined the shelf above.

Some of her best inventions looked back at her. First were the Shh!-Oos. Now *they* would definitely come in handy. She had made the super sneaky invention after weeks of searching for the perfect, sound-absorbing material. Eventually, she'd found a leaf in the forest that seemed to absorb nearly all sound once it had been shredded, bound tightly together, and interwoven with tree roots. She'd packed it into a metal frame and attached the frames to her shoes. Even Ember had to admit, it was one of her best inventions. The soles let her creep around completely unnoticed.

Next, she picked up the Nothing-Goes-Bump-In-The-Light that she had built for Juniper. It hadn't been used for a few months now, not since her sister overcame her fear of the dark. It was simple, a jar filled with luminescent plants. When you shook the jar, the plants would glow with a bright light for twelve hours, slowly dimming until they were shaken again, charged up by the energy of the movement. Probably another sensible thing to take.

But the self-stirring pot and spoon she had built for Mum, named Stir Potsalot by Juniper, would be no good. Nor would the table leg extenders, or the system of wires and tin cans she had built to let her and Juniper talk through their bedroom walls. There was the quill, though: Auto-Quill Inkorporated. She had worked on it for months and months, desperately trying to get it to write without anyone holding it. She had attached wheels to the base on either side of the tip, and there was an inkpot strapped to the feather, as well as a tiny solar panel to power it. At last, it had been able to draw a straight line unaided. But then Ms Daylands had seen it in action, and she warned Ember not to make inventions that might be considered dangerous.

Dangerous. She rolled her eyes. Good. *A little danger might be helpful on this trip*, she thought, carefully putting it into the bag.

There, at the bottom of the bag, was the bookrest for Juniper. As Ember reached in to take it out, she changed her mind. She'd take it with her, then, when she got back and everything was fixed, she'd finally give it to Juniper and everything would feel normal again.

After that, Ember added a few essentials – her toolkit from Dad, some scrap pieces of metal, screws, nuts, a packet of matches – and attached the Shh!-Oos to the bottom of her boots. Once she had everything ready, she stood at the door and scouted the rest of the room to make sure she hadn't forgotten anything. Time to go.

She clicked the switch on the wall and the light bulbs all flickered off.

Ember tiptoed into the hall towards Juniper's room. So far, the shoes were working as they should. The next step would be tricky though; Juniper's door always creaked at a certain point. She inched it open a crack, waited for her eyes to adjust to the darkness, and squeezed through. She had to find the card.

The sound of Juniper's breathing filled her ears as Ember crept around the bed, searching everywhere.

There. A tiny corner of the card was peeking out from under Juniper's pillow. The same hiding spot Ember herself had used. They really were like two froghoppers on a single lily pad. Carefully, slowly, she gripped the card and gently tugged. It was out.

Back in the hallway, Ember let her hands brush

the wall of Juniper's bedroom, a silent promise that she would do whatever she could, and then she left the house into the night air.

*

Ember found her way through the roundhouses and all the way to the edge of the village in complete silence. It was cold now, and she was glad she had worn her winter jacket zipped right up to her chin. The Shh!-Oos had worked exactly as she had hoped. There were a few weeds tangled up in the soles from crossing the field between the houses and where the mountain began, but she had done it.

Mount Never. Standing before her was an iron arch made from tangled threads of metal that wormed their way from the ground to the top like tree roots in reverse. At the top, they joined together to form the mountain's name. The arch marked the start of a brick-paved path which snaked around the edge of the mountain, overgrown weeds pushing between its cracks.

Ember allowed herself one look back at the village. She had always loved the way Everspring was nestled between forests and mountains. It felt safe, cosy; it felt

like home. But it hadn't felt so safe recently, not since Juniper's card had arrived.

She had made up her mind. Too late to turn back now.

She stepped on to the path. Only one foot to begin with, in case – well, she wasn't really sure what might happen, but just to be sure.

Nothing happened. She took another step, and then another, and another. She was doing it. She was climbing the mountain! But before she had time to feel impressed with her own confidence, a fog descended, thickening with every one of her strides. In a moment, the village behind her was hidden in the smog, and she couldn't see more than a few feet in front of her.

She slowed. On the right side of the path, crooked trees twisted among each other before disappearing into the white mist.

She could do this. It was just a mountain. Magical, yes, but—

'Excuse me, ma'am?'

Ember shrieked, spinning round to face the voice behind her.

'Over here.'

Her heart stopped and she froze, eyes wide. There was a man sitting in a wooden chair on the edge of the path. She must have walked straight past him.

She blinked. 'I, you, I mean, who are—'

The man, who was wearing grey overalls with a matching grey cap, slapped his hands on his knees and pushed himself up.

'Name's Flint,' he said, holding out his hand as he stepped on to the path. 'Nice to meet ya.'

Ember couldn't hide her surprise. She hadn't expected to find anyone else on the mountain after what Ms Daylands had said. But here, so close to the village, was Flint, who seemed old enough to be her dad, with pale skin slightly wrinkled around a pair of bright blue eyes. Dark grey wisps of hair poked out from beneath his cap, curling at the ends.

'I didn't think there was anyone on the mountain,' Ember finally managed to say, once she'd recovered from the shock.

'Yeah, it's just been me for – well, a while.'

'Who are you? How did you get here?'

'I'm Flint. I said that already. It's actually *you* who hasn't said much.'

'Right,' she said. 'I'm Ember.' She tried to think how to politely ask what she wanted to know. 'Ms Daylands told me no one had ever climbed the mountain. So I wasn't expecting to see anyone. Erm, have you?'

'Have I what?'

'Climbed the mountain!'

'Hard t'say.'

'If you're not here to climb the mountain, why are you here?' Ember tried again.

'You're a nosy one, ain't ya? I'm the Mountain Keeper. Here to make sure everyone knows where they're going.'

'Erm, well isn't that obvious? I'm going up.'

Flint's face contorted, eyes wide as if he'd seen a ghost. He waved his hands at Ember and she stepped back again. 'No, no, no!' he shouted.

'But I—'

'Why would you want to go up there? No one climbs this mountain, no one!'

'Well, I—'

'That's mad, ma'am.'

'Can you let me—'

'No! No, no, no, no!'

He kept on talking, interrupting Ember every time she tried to explain. So she stood, arms folded, and waited. Finally, when Flint was out of breath, he stopped.

'I'm going up,' Ember said again.

'Young lady,' he said, hands on his hips. 'Don't you know what happens to people once they step on this mountain?'

'They lose their fate. But . . .' she said, narrowing her eyes, '*you're* on the mountain, and you're fine!'

Flint looked at her and raised one eyebrow. He readjusted his cap and peered up the path, then back to Ember. 'That's a good point you make. But that's different.'

'Different how?'

'None o' your business.'

'Are you magic?'

'I said, none o' your business.'

He doesn't look very magic, Ember thought.

'Look,' said Ember. 'I'm going up because I made a promise and I won't be giving up before I've even started.' She straightened her back. 'Please move aside.'

Flint looked like someone had slapped him across the face. 'Now, listen here. You don't want to get stuck in those realms up on this mountain. Terrifying places.'

'If they're so terrifying, why don't you leave?' she asked.

'Told you – it's none o' your business.'

As he spoke, something caught Ember's eye.

Behind Flint, a tiny shape was floating closer to them, and Ember could see the familiar silhouette of a small, folded bird. Her stomach twisted.

'Don't. Move,' she whispered, as it flew right towards Flint.

'What you talking about?' he asked, spinning round as the bird nipped past his ear. He leapt into the air, cowering behind Ember, while the paper bird settled on the back of the chair.

'Bad omens, them,' he hissed in her ear. 'Haven't seen one for years.'

He could see the bird! Relief exploded inside Ember. She wasn't imagining things. It was still a bad omen of course, but even so, knowing she wasn't imagining it was comforting somehow.

The bird looked exactly like the others, an origami body with very real, reflective eyes, which were staring right at her. She stepped forward, feeling more confident now that she knew it was real. The bird's head tilted, ever so slightly, and her skin prickled.

Omens were supposed to be warnings, but the birds never seemed to be trying to tell her something. No . . . with their spooky silence, their strange long beaks, their blinking, darting eyes, it felt as though they were there to *watch* her.

Another step forward, and the bird flew off, flapping its tiny wings as it darted up the side of the mountain and into the trees.

Flint popped out from behind her. 'You're bad news you are, young lady. You need to go.'

She turned around and faced the path. 'Fine. I'll be leaving then.'

'Woah, woah, woah,' said Flint, hopping in front of her again. 'If you really are going up the mountain, *against* my advice, I might add, I'll be needing some sort of Mountain Keeper payment.'

'Payment?'

He nodded, looking her up and down. 'I'll take them shoes.'

She looked down at her feet. 'No way. I need these.'

Flint shifted his weight to one leg and folded his arms. 'Mountain Keepers need paying.'

'What about if I pay you with something else that I brought with me?' Ember suggested.

'What you got?'

'A light that never goes out?'

'Like the sun? No thanks.'

Ember bristled. 'OK, how about a quill that can write by itself?'

'I've got hands.'

'A bookstand?'

'No books.'

She glared at him. What kind of person didn't have books?

Ember didn't want to give up the Shh!-Oos, especially to someone who had made fun of her inventions. But it didn't seem as if she had much choice. She had to get up the mountain and he was wasting her time. Flint was still eyeing her feet like a wolf ready to pounce.

'Fine,' she said, unclipping the soles from her shoes. 'Take them.'

He grinned, snatching them from her like a child as soon as she held them out. 'Very kind of you,' he said. 'And don't say I didn't warn you about what's ahead: lots of realms, lots of magic, lots of danger.'

He turned back to his chair and sat down to inspect his prize.

'And stay away from them birds!' he called after her, as he began to attach the soles to his shoes.

Ember took a deep breath, and started to walk. She wondered what dangerous magic she might find. Maybe something that turned her into a statue, or made her disappear into a puff of wind, or wiped her memory . . .

But whatever was up there, it had to be less scary than having an empty Fate Card, and *much* less scary than the thought of what was going to happen to her sister.

Whatever is up there, it will be worth it to save Juniper, she told herself.

She just hoped she wasn't wrong.

7

Ember followed the path higher and higher into the strange fog. It seemed to cling to her skin and stick to her clothes, more like smoke than any kind of fog she had seen. It was eerie. Not that she was scared. No. Just, well, *careful*. Cautious.

To her right, the mountainside was covered in a tangle of shrubs and moss-covered trees, while to the left was empty air, the rocky edge of the mountain path at her feet barely visible in the grey fog. She clutched her backpack straps and focused on the ground beneath her feet. Every step seemed to echo loudly now, thanks to Flint.

Suddenly, the mist grew thicker, much thicker. Clouds of it swirled around her, and a damp, musty smell hung in the air. She reached out into the whiteness, and when she pulled her hand back, the fog had stuck to her skin like spider webs.

Ember walked on, and the strands pulling at her became tougher, stringier, until it felt like she was wading through marshmallow. With every step, the mist pulled harder. It tugged at her shoulders, wrenched at the back of her hair, dragged at her feet.

Panic started to build in her chest. Was this what Flint had meant about *getting stuck*? The fog pulled at everything: her lips, her jaw, even her teeth, until she was motionless, gripped by thick clouds of sticky white. No, she couldn't get stuck so soon! *Push! Come on, Ember, push!*

This couldn't be the end of her journey already. She set her jaw. She wouldn't let it be.

She forced one step, and then another. And then, with one last push, Ember burst through the clouds, stumbling to the ground. Relief washed over her as she bent forward and gasped for air. It was like surfacing from underwater, her lungs burning and struggling with every breath.

When Ember stood and looked around, her breathing back to its familiar rhythm, what she saw almost made her fall down all over again.

Everything had changed.

The usually distant moon that had been hidden by fog only moments ago now hung so close and so bright that she could make out the lines of craters. It was as if someone had looped a rope around it and heaved it as near to the world as they could without blocking out the sky altogether.

But that wasn't all. She was now standing on the edge of a huge forest, the length of it stretching as far as she could see to both her left and right, with a narrow path down the middle. The mountain footpath, the mossy trees, the tangled shrubs – they had all disappeared.

This must have been what Flint and Ms Daylands had been talking about – realms and magic. A moon that big . . . well, there was no other explanation. Ember pulled the straps of her bag tighter and swallowed. There was no other way to go, and there was no way she was going back through that horrible marshmallow fog now. She had to do this. She had to. Otherwise Juniper would run out of time. Ember would be miserable for ever. Dad would have died for nothing.

So, with a deep breath, Ember stepped forward.

The trees on the outside of the forest, lining its border, had looked perfectly uniform. But once she stepped into the woods she realised that each tree was unique. Some were twisted, some tall, there was one with pale pink blossoms, and another with huge roots that spread across the forest floor.

Then, Ember noticed the noise. A thousand ticking sounds filled her ears like a wave of butterfly wings, all flapping at different speeds, keeping their own rhythm in the symphony. But as she edged towards the closest tree, a tall oak with leaves bigger than her hands, she realised it wasn't the sound of wings at all.

The thick branches stretched out, and hanging from the lowest one was an old, antique clock. Ember had never seen one quite like it. The ivory clock face was framed in a beautiful copper box with a matching handle. Etched leaf patterns crept up the sides of the box like ivy, winding their way around the circular face. There were two copper clock hands, each one with a leaf-shaped end pointing to a number. Above, the name *Filbert Gnarlsworth* was scratched into the copper.

As Ember moved closer to get a better look, she realised the clock had thirteen numbers equally spaced out on its face; a zero was placed between the twelve and one. The longer of the two hands pointed to six and the shorter to four. It couldn't be 6:20 already, could it? She had left the house at midnight. The clock must be wrong, or maybe time was different here. They certainly didn't have zeros on clocks in Everspring.

Ember walked to the next tree. It was a cherry blossom and, on the ground below, thousands of pale pink petals had gathered like a carpet of candyfloss snow. Hanging above, on one of its long, thin branches, was a miniature grandfather clock made of dark brown wood. The two hands pointed to seven and eight. *Strange*, Ember thought. *Why would it tell a different time to the first?*

But as she continued through the forest, she discovered clocks hanging in every single tree, each one a different design or style, and each one telling a different time. There was a pine tree with a watch fastened around a narrow bough, a tall tree with huge knobbly branches and an enormous clock resting against its trunk, and a small sapling with a tiny stopwatch threaded around its sprouting limbs. Ember walked past tree after tree, clock after clock, each with its own rhythm, filling the forest with an orchestra of ticks and tocks.

Ember had the sense that something was pulling her forward. It was hard to put her finger on what, exactly. It wasn't the Fixer's Feeling, not quite; it was more like instinct, something deep inside showing her the way. And then she saw it.

A magnificent tree stood further along the path, its tall, strong trunk erupting into golden orange. The colour seemed to burn on the edges of its almond-shaped leaves, smouldering like the last flames of a fire. It shone out like a beacon, illuminated by the moonlight.

Ember had no idea what kind of tree it was, but she ran towards it, magnetised, ducking under the canopy of branches to reach the centre. Carved into the trunk was a hole, and inside the hole, was the clock. It was unique, of course, like the others, and the pull that had carried Ember here finally stopped as she laid her hand on its face.

It was breathtaking. A delicate circular glass case housed hundreds of cogs, ticking round as they clicked into one another, all the mechanics of the clock entirely exposed. She could see every spring, every nut. On the front were two silver hands, one slightly longer than the other, and thirteen numbers. Right at the top was her name, etched into the glass. *Ember Shadows*.

But something was wrong. As she went to pick the clock up, the hands spun around, paused for a second, and then moved again. She peered closer, gently lifting the clock away from the hole, and turned it over.

Etched into the back of the glass case was a number – fifty – but it disappeared almost immediately, to be rewritten, stroke by stroke, as if some invisible person were scratching it out in front of her. Seventeen, seventy-two, thirty-four, forty-eight. It wouldn't stay on one number.

Just then, a voice sounded from behind her.

'Ember Shadows? Is that you?'

8

Ember spun round. At first, she didn't see anyone.

'Ember Shadows?' the voice asked again.

Her heart hammering a thousand times a second, Ember lowered her eyes to where the voice was coming from.

There, standing in front of her was . . . well, she didn't really know *what* it was. It definitely didn't look like an animal. It was the same sort of height as a rabbit on its hind legs, and was very thin, with turned-out feet. Its arms were even thinner than its legs and . . . were those tiny little hands, resting around its middle? The creature was completely naked and a funny metallic dark grey colour. But the strangest part of it had to be its bizarre shape. Its long thin body bulged out to form a head, which then narrowed into a point at the top, like a leaf. And it was beaming up at her with what was possibly the friendliest, toothiest, tiniest smile she could imagine.

'Well?' the creature asked excitedly, as he waddled forward. '*Are* you?'

Ember blinked. Staring at him, she'd totally forgotten he'd said anything.

'Oh, erm. Yes, I'm Ember.'

His stuck-out feet pushed off the ground and he leapt into the air, whooping and cheering as he zipped around her as high as her head.

'Oh, you can't imagine how happy I am to meet you. What an honour, a real honour, and at your own tree! Well, I should have guessed really, I should have imagined that's where you'd be.'

With a final twirl, he landed back on the forest floor and then hurried towards her, his right arm outstretched. Ember hesitated for a second, and then lowered down on to her knees. She held out her hand and he gripped her index finger with both of his tiny hands and shook, so hard she thought he might break it.

'Hans,' he said, bowing his head towards her. 'At your service.'

'Hans?' She looked down at him. 'Ohhh, *hands*. I get it.'

'Get what?' His wide eyes stared up at her from his flat face. 'It's *Hans*, not hands.'

'Yes, but you're a . . . well, you're a clock hand, aren't you?'

He let go of her finger and stepped back a couple of paces. Maybe she shouldn't have said that. Slowly, he looked down at himself, then back at her. 'Yes. So?'

'I thought maybe that's why you were named—'

Before she knew it, he had folded over, bent some invisible knees, and was exploding with laughter. 'Oh Ember Shadows, what a funny one you are! Did you really think that all hands were called Hans? I suppose you're the leftovers of a fire, are you? Are you a pile of embers?'

'No, I just thought—'

'Do you crackle when you sleep?'

She glared at him then and waited for him to stop laughing. It wasn't even that funny.

'Oh, I'm so sorry, Ember Shadows. It's just, you can't imagine how excited I am to meet you. Your name has been rustling in the leaves for weeks.'

'My name?'

'Of course! Why wouldn't it be? Look at that clock of yours.'

Ember glanced back over her shoulder. The hands of the glass clock were still spinning round, settling on two numbers for a moment and then spinning round again.

'It's my clock? I mean, I saw my name, but – wait, what's wrong with it?'

'Wrong? Nothing at all. It's right, that's what's so exciting!'

He ran past her and towards the tree, leaping up and down as he went shooting into the sky, like a firework.

'Ember Shadows, the great Ember Shadows,' he said. He jumped forward and clung to the tree like a monkey before sliding down to the bottom.

Ember couldn't help laughing at him as he smiled, eyes closed, hugging the trunk like it was the greatest thing he'd ever seen.

'My goodness. How rude of me,' he said, landing on his feet as if he'd just remembered something. He bounced back over to her. With one hand across his chest – or where a person might have a chest – he cleared his throat and closed his eyes. 'I, Hans, pledge my absolute whole life to you, Ember Shadows. I will be the most helpful hand you have ever seen, I will be the most loyal friend on your quest, the most useful colleague on your journey, the best cog in the machine of life, the greatest—'

'Woah, wait a second,' said Ember. Hans opened his eyes. 'My quest? You mean saving Juniper?'

Hans looked confused. 'Aren't you here to fix the mountain?'

'Fix the mountain? No, I'm here to save my sister, Juniper. And I want to find a fate, if I can.'

He frowned. At least, it *looked* like a frown; his eyebrows were such small etches on the metal that it was hard to tell. 'Maybe it's all part of the same problem then,' he said, with a shrug.

'What's wrong with the mountain? What are these clocks? And what is this place anyway?'

'Well, Ember Shadows—'

'Can you just call me Ember?'

'Of course, Ember.' He then mouthed her surname silently and winked as though they had shared a joke. 'Take a seat.'

Ember sat cross-legged under the tree and Hans began to pace in front of her. 'This is the Forest of Time,' he said grandly.

He paused and Ember nodded impatiently at him to go on.

He gave an excited little hop and continued. 'Every tree here is connected to someone in your world. When you die, the tree dies with you. But the tree will not die until the time set on your clock. It's fate. So if a clock is set to nine and three, that person will die at the ripe old age of ninety-three. What a fine age to shrivel up and die. To be buried under the ground like a seed. Such a wonderful age to have the life sucked from—'

'Like on the cards!' Ember interrupted.

'What cards?'

She thought of showing him Juniper's, but he finally seemed to be getting to the point and she didn't want to distract him. 'Oh, never mind,' she said. 'Keep going.'

He smiled and sat down, crossing his legs as she had done. Then he pointed at his legs and then to hers, giggling like it was another funny joke they had made.

'So a long, long, long, long—'

'Hans!'

'Right, sorry. A long time ago – even before I became full of fabulous life and was nothing more than a piece of metal – the clocks all used to be like yours. They would change all the time. Every time someone made a decision, it changed when they might die. But slowly, over the years, the clocks began freezing. They were getting stuck, staying on one number for ever.' He shook his head sadly.

'Why did the clocks start freezing?' Ember asked.

'Well . . .' he started, whispering as though he were about to share a secret, '*I* think it's something to do with the Threads of Fate.'

'Threads?'

'Mmm. Long ago, threads used to shoot up and down and all over this mountain, moving around as people made their decisions. They'd loop-the-loop through this realm and the next, back and forth, picking up bits of this and that as people changed their minds.'

'What stopped them?'

Hans shrugged his tiny shoulders and sighed. 'Hard to say. I can't remember much about my days as a thing.'

He bounced up and halted in mid-air, hovering directly in front of Ember's face, inches from her nose.

'You see, I'm . . .' he paused, sounding almost ashamed, '. . . a spare part. Tragic, really. Such talent, gone to waste. I could have pointed at any number, any number you'd like. See?' He twisted and turned in the air as if proving a point, showing off all the angles he could tilt to, before he sank to the ground like a fallen leaf. 'But there's no clock for me. No clock for little old Hans.'

He looked glum, and something chimed inside Ember. She knew how it felt to be a spare part when everything else worked in such perfect harmony.

'Where are all the other spare parts?' she asked. 'There must be more like you?'

Hans looked down to his crossed legs. 'It's only been me, for as long as I can remember. But I bet there are others, spare parts from other clocks, who have soaked up the forest's magic like I did. They're probably all thinking, walking, talking wonders like me!' He leant forward, hands cupped around his tiny mouth in a whisper. 'I bet it's the biggest game of hide and seek, and they're waiting for me to jump out and find them. Just you wait, one day . . .'

Ember blinked at the idea of *more* Hanses. But then, a bolt of energy shot through her like a lightning streak. Juniper's clock. It must be here, it had to be. If she could find Juniper's clock, maybe she could change it – and change her fate.

'Hans, I need your help. I need—'

'Wooooooohheeeeeoooooooo.' He shot into the air, pirouetting around as he released a shriek. 'Help is my middle name.'

'Great, I need you to—'

'Actually, I don't have a middle name, or an end name.'

'That's OK, I need—'

'You're right, who needs a middle name when you've got a friend like the marvellous Ember Shadows! I'll help you until the end of time!'

'Well I don't need help until the end of time, I can do everything else on my own, I just need—'

'The end of time. For ever. Until the end. Always.'

'Hans, please!'

'Right,' he said, winking at her again. 'Let me give you a helping hand.'

Ember rolled her eyes as he fought to hold in the laughter.

'Forget it,' she said, pulling her bag on to her back and getting to her feet. She could find Juniper's tree herself.

'No, wait! I can help, wait for me. Wait!'

Ember could see him out of the corner of her eye as he waddled after her, hopping and leaping to keep up.

The plan was back in action.

9

It didn't take them long to find Juniper's tree.

'Are you sure this is it?' Ember asked.

'Excuse me,' said Hans, sounding offended. 'I know every tree in this forest and this is absolutely the one and only Juniper tree. Well it's not a *juniper* tree, but it is called Juniper!' He stifled a laugh.

It was actually a mulberry tree. Ember had seen them in the forest near her treehouse. This one was still young, but it had black and red berries growing from its branches beneath bright green leaves. As she got closer, she could see silkworms climbing up the trunk, and a hole higher up with what looked like a bird's nest tucked inside.

'Does your sister, by any chance, like animals?' said Hans.

'She *loves* them. She likes to help sick ones. Once she found a squirrel with a broken leg and kept it in a cardboard box in her room until it had recovered.'

Hans nodded. 'That explains it. Although I've never seen an animal like that in this forest before.'

She followed his pointing hand to a branch above their heads where a white bird sat, staring down at them. Another omen. She stepped closer, moving towards it, bravery building with each step. It didn't fly away like the other one had, but seemed to stare *more* intently at her, challenging her to look away first.

Then a second one appeared, darting down from a higher branch, joining the first. Ember swallowed, her bravery vanishing. She had never seen more than one at a time before.

The two birds moved in perfect unison, their paper wings synchronised as they folded into their bodies. Maybe it was what Ms Daylands had said, or the silent way they moved, or the fact they weren't trying to hide themselves from others any more, but they seemed spookier up here.

'Strange,' she whispered.

At the sound of her voice, the birds flew up into the tree and behind the leaves, so that Ember could no longer see them. Still, she could feel them watching her.

She took a deep breath, stepped forward, and laid her hand on the trunk of Juniper's tree. The tree didn't feel like it was dying; it didn't even look old. A clock lay on the floor, fastened around the trunk by a silver chain. It was a pocket watch, small enough to hold in the palm of her hand. The longer hand pointed to zero, and the shorter one to eight. Ember turned it over, the beats ticking away at her skin, but she already knew what would be on the other side. A silver eight. It was like the number scratched into her own, except this one didn't change at all. It stayed put, stubbornly insisting on her sister's looming death.

She tried twisting the knob on the top of the clock to change the time. The hands didn't move, but she hadn't expected it to be that easy. It shouldn't be too hard to fix though. She'd worked on hundreds of clocks down in the village, how different could it be?

Hans started humming as Ember pulled the bag off her back and opened up her silver toolbox. She would need her smallest screwdriver and a pair of tweezers.

Carefully, she flipped over the pocket watch and began unscrewing the back. It came away easily, lifting up like a flap to reveal the inner workings. The insides of a clock were always inspiring; every part worked in harmony, every spring and wheel and cog ticked away perfectly together, like the best kind of team. And every part had an important job.

'Ember, what are you—'

'Shh, I need to concentrate,' Ember said, peering closer at the inner workings.

She spotted the hour wheel and the minute wheel. Of course, they weren't hours and minutes up here, but the mechanisms seemed the same. One was bigger than the other, but both had tiny teeth all the way around the outsides. Neither of them moved, but something behind the next layer of casing was clearly turning around, ticking away as the clock worked.

Ember gripped the tweezers and tried to steady her hand. It was important that she did this right, especially with such a small clock. One slip and she could – no. She couldn't think like that. She clasped the tweezers around the tiny teeth of the hour wheel and twisted, turning the circle. Careful, careful. She pulled away and turned the clock over.

With a sigh, Ember realised she had turned the wrong hand. The shorter hand, the one that had been pointing to eight, was now on nine. That wasn't enough. She'd have to turn the other one if she wanted Juniper to have more than only one extra year.

The tweezers gripped the teeth of the second wheel.

'Ember, do you know what—'

'Hans, I know what I'm doing. Zip it.'

He pretended to zip his lips and Ember tried to ignore his worried face. She tucked her hair behind her ears and went back to the wheels. This time, she held Juniper's clock so she could see the longer hand turn as she worked, past the four, past the six, all the way to eight.

Eighty-nine. She smiled. Everyone would agree, eighty-nine was a good age to—

Pop.

Clunk.

'That didn't sound good,' said Hans.

One of the two silver wheels had snapped in half.

Ember turned the clock over, her heart hammering against her ribs. A black hole seemed to open up in her stomach when she saw the front. The two hands hung limply from the centre, both pointing to the bottom of the clock face.

'No, no, no, no!' she gasped. 'That wasn't meant to happen.'

'I thought you knew what you were d-d-doing, a-a- and my lips were z-z-zipped!' Hans said, stammering.

As Hans spoke, the hands on Juniper's clock stiffened, and began to whizz around the numbers, spinning in opposite directions. They flew around the circle again and again, until suddenly, they stopped.

One hand was pointing at the twelve. One was pointing at the three.

'Uh-oh,' whispered Hans.

'That means 123, right?' Ember gulped, hoping she was right, though she already knew from Hans' voice that something was very wrong. 'Juniper will live to 123?'

Hans shook his head. 'Look.' He stepped forward and pushed the back casing of the clock into place. With a tiny finger, he pointed to where the eight had been scratched into the silver. Now in its place were the numbers 03:00.

Ember watched as the digits were wiped off the back and, stroke by stroke, something new appeared:

02:59. Her heart clenched.

The clock ticked, each second drumming in her ears. It had stopped predicting an age of death. Now, it was doing something else . . .

'It's counting down?'

'I'm sorry, Ember Shadows,' Hans said softly. 'I wanted to tell you but I zipped my lips before the words could come out.' He waddled back to the path, the tip of his head bowed.

'Wait, Hans! What do I do?' asked Ember desperately. Her hands were shaking. 'What's it counting down to?'

But she already knew the answer.

'Juniper's death, of course.' Hans turned towards her, his hands on his head in misery. 'Oh, it's all my fault. I knew it. I knew it. I don't know *how* I knew it. But I knew . . .'

'Hans, you're not making any sense!'

'You see, taking a hand *off* the clock can stop you ever growing old. Imagine that! Bam! Stuck at age eight for ever. What an age.'

'But moving the hands?' Ember asked.

Hans hesitated. 'I don't think it's ever been done

before. But a clock can't last long with broken parts, that's for sure. This one only has three hours – oh no, two hours and fifty-nine minutes – left.'

'Three hours? But I don't even have a plan!'

What had she done? She should have left the clock alone!

'We had better get a move on, I'd say, and I'll keep my lips fully unzipped from now on. You should probably bring *that* with us.' Hans pointed at the clock.

'Bring it where?'

'Up the mountain! This mountain is chock-a-block full of magical realms! I bet one of them will have exactly the magic we need to fix it!'

'But, Hans,' Ember said, an idea forming, 'we're in a forest full of clocks already! Can't I take a wheel from a clock here and use that to fix Juniper's clock?'

Hans stared at her, his eyes wide. 'You want to steal someone else's time? The great Ember Shadows? Killing someone else to save your sister?'

She cringed and looked down. No. She couldn't. She wasn't that person.

'You will need a new wheel to fix the clock,' continued Hans, drumming his chin thoughtfully with his tiny fingers. 'But if we *only* replace the wheel, that will probably just give her the number eight again. We'll also need some *seriously* super magic if we're going to give her extra years.'

He turned on his tiny feet and started bouncing along the path, further into the forest.

'But how do you know we'll find the right magic? Or a new wheel?' Ember called after him. Finding one of these items seemed like it would be hard enough, but *both* of them? 'There can't be clock wheels all over the mountain, can there?'

Hans shrugged. 'I don't know. But *I'm* a spare part. Surely there are more spare parts somewhere? Like that big game of hide and seek! We just have to find them, and then get hold of some magic!'

Ember hoped he was right.

She had already made everything worse, and she had only just started her journey. With nowhere else to go, she gathered up Juniper's clock and pulled it from the chain on the tree. Carefully, she placed it inside her toolbox.

But as she went to close the box, the number on the back of the clock faded, and a new one appeared.

02:58

If they were going to find a new wheel *and* some powerful magic, they were going to have to hurry.

10

The pair rushed along the path through the seemingly never-ending forest and Hans would *not* stop talking. Not even for a millisecond. It was as though he didn't understand how terrifying this had become. The cards in Ember's bag had been scary enough, but now, with her sister's broken clock counting down to her death just hours away, things had become much more urgent.

They approached the edge of the forest. She could see the trees beginning to thin and another wall of white marshmallow-fog stretching up to the bright night sky. She slowed down to ready herself for whatever might be on the other side.

'I just want you to tell me what I can do,' Hans prattled on. 'So that we can be *best friends for ever.*'

'Hans, can you *please* stop talking for a little bit?' Ember said. 'Anyway, you can't be best friends for ever with someone you've just met. You have to get to know each other.'

'Of course you can. It's called friends at first sight.' He was still bouncing along beside her, like a spring.

'Well, I've already got a best friend. My sister. But I have to fix her clock.'

'And I'm the friend to help you. Until the end of time.'

I should have left him under her tree, Ember thought. She could do this on her own.

'You know,' Hans whispered, cutting into her train of thought. 'I've never left this forest before. Not in all my years of being here.'

'How old *are* you?' Ember asked, curious in spite of herself.

'I really don't know. I *do* remember being trapped and stuck. I was just a thing. Then I woke up here one day, with hands of my own. My memories from before are all misty, blurry things.'

'And you've never left the forest?'

'Never. This is the best day of my life.'

Ember sighed. 'OK, but if you are coming, you've got to be careful. I can't wait for you if you get into trouble. I haven't got time.'

'Don't you worry, Ember Shadows. I am a speed wizard. I *am* time! I can move in fast forward.' He started laughing at his own joke before he even finished his sentence.

Ember picked him up and tucked him inside her jacket, zipping up the bottom so he could cling on to the zip and poke his head out under hers.

'Onwards.' He pointed his arm towards the dreaded fog.

*

The mist wasn't quite as bad the second time, but it still left Ember panting and Hans flat out on the floor. He looked exhausted, even though she was the one who had fought through the white sticky stuff for both of them.

She hadn't thought it was possible, but the moon hung even closer now, the curve of it dipping towards her in the inky black night sky. Once again, she was standing on the edge of a realm, but rather than trees lining the border, now bookshelves towered up towards the sky, stretching out to the horizon on both the left and right. Books on a mountain. She couldn't help but smile. It was both bizarre and wonderful at the same time.

She sprinted forward to an opening in the shelves, and, with an excited squeal, entered the colossal library.

'It's like a rainbow,' whispered Hans as he stared up at the colourful spines gleaming out at them.

A noise grew above them, almost like a gentle clapping sound. From the depths of the book world, a shape emerged.

'Is that . . . is that a flying book?' said Ember.

It was. She had to blink to make sure she wasn't dreaming. But there it was, the covers flapping like wings and the pages rustling beneath as the book flew through the sky, before it closed itself, hung in the air for a moment, and then slotted itself into a space on the shelf.

'Look, another one,' said Hans.

Every few seconds, a book leapt from its place on a shelf and flew away, or one flew into view to push itself into an empty slot. They were all shapes and sizes, some tiny books zipping through the sky like robins, others heavy and fat like chickens, barely able to keep a few feet off the floor. It was truly magical. And the best part, Ember thought as she breathed in, was the

unmistakable smell, her absolute favourite smell in the
world – new books. Despite her terror over the
countdown towards Juniper's death, for a second, she
felt comforted.

'I think I'm going to like this realm,' she said,
smiling down at Hans. 'Come on. There might be a
spare part here, or maybe a book that can help me fix
Juniper's clock.'

The pair of them hurried forward, eyes searching
the thousands of titles that stared out at them. Some of
them Ember had read or lent to Juniper – *Alyssia
in Wonderland*, *Petra Pan*, *The Wind in the*

Wilderness – but there were others she'd never heard of. She strained her neck to see some of the higher shelves. There was no ladder to reach them but she realised it wasn't needed; the books were organising themselves. Each book seemed to know when it was needed and it would leave and fly away – although where they went, Ember wasn't sure. Other books were returning to their places on the shelves, swooping down from above when they reached the right spot.

Hans seemed to be in a sort of shock. He hadn't bounced a single time since they had made it through the fog. His eyes were wide, his tiny mouth hanging open as he stared up at the flying books. Catching Ember's eye, he grinned and then rocketed into the air, returning to his usual self.

'Wooooooopppeeeeyyyyy! Can you believe it, Ember? I'm out of the Forest of Time! And look at that! Have you seen this one? Ember, look, this one's purple. I think purple's my favourite colour now.'

The books seemed wary of Hans and Ember. Some shuddered as they neared, others darted away like startled birds. Two jumped from the shelves and flapped around their heads, and one even caused such a commotion that a whole shelf fell on to the floor.

Suddenly, Hans stopped, arms and legs outstretched as far as they went, as if he were trying to make a star shape. His mouth open, he slapped his hands against his head and turned slowly to Ember.

'What? What is it?' she asked anxiously. Could he have found something that would help?

'This one. It's got my name on it! I'm famous!'

He prodded a book on the second shelf. Ember peered at the spine.

'See?' Hans went on. *Hans Christof Sanderson.* I

don't know those other two, but Hans, that's me!' He prodded the spine and the book shuffled and sprang out of the shelf, flying away from its attacker towards a top shelf, out of their reach. 'I'm famous! Do you think that book is all about my wonderful life and all the amazing things I've done? I wonder if it tells the story about the time I made up that dance in the forest!'

'No, silly,' said Ember, trying to push aside the disappointment of not finding the magic or spare part they needed. 'Hans Christof Sanderson is one person. He used to write tales about all the places in the world you could find magic.'

Hans' face dropped, the smile that had been plastered across it gone in a second. 'So what you're telling me, is someone has taken my name?'

'No, it's someone—'

'The horror! Oh, Ember this is terrible news.' He began to pace up and down, clutching his head in his hands. 'How do I get my name back? What will I be called? Oh dear, oh dear, this is not good. How could he take my name? Do you know, I never even felt it go?'

'No, Hans! You're still Hans,' said Ember. 'He has

the same name as you, that's all.'

He stopped and narrowed his tiny eyes.

'The same name? Interesting. What about you, Ember? Does anyone have the same name as you?'

They started walking again. 'Maybe,' said Ember. 'I don't think so, though. Ember isn't really a name, not normally. My dad chose it.'

'Why would he choose a name that isn't a name?'

'He said when I was born, my hair looked like burning embers, and he knew right at that moment that I was made to start a fire.' She smiled, remembering the way he would ruffle her hair whenever he told the story, his hands coarse from working on his latest creation.

'Well, that seems very dangerous,' said Hans, sounding shocked. 'I hope he wore protective equipment when he held you.'

'No, he meant like a *metaphorical* fire.'

Hans looked confused.

'He meant I was born to change something – like how the ember of one old fire can start a whole new one.' She looked down at Hans, who seemed to be trying to understand what she meant. 'It's like when my sister was born they named her Juniper, because Dad said her eyes were a blue as deep as the colour of juniper berries. He didn't mean her eyes were *actually* berries though.'

Hans still looked bewildered.

'Never mind,' Ember said with a sigh. 'It's just something my dad used to say.'

'Well, maybe he should have called you Map because directions would be more helpful than a fire right now. Which way do we go?'

Hans was right. There was a fork in the road, and two identical paths lined with bookshelves lay before them, one heading left, the other right.

'Hans, I think this is a maze.' Ember looked back, but the path where they had entered had been closed off, replaced by a wall of books. 'Not just a maze, it's a *moving* maze.'

Her eyes scanned the path and panic started to rise as she suddenly realised they were trapped. 'How are we meant to know which way to go? I can't see any spare parts or anything to help us fix Juniper's clock in here, and we'll run out of time if we can't get through the maze quickly!'

They stood, staring at the two paths ahead. Ember

was just about to make a decision, when a low, slow voice broke the silence.

'Maybe I can help?'

11

Ember looked down at Hans, but he stared back up at her and shrugged. If neither of them had spoken, who had?

They both turned, searching for the voice's owner.

'Over here,' it droned. 'Right in front of you, for goodness' sake.'

Ember peered down the two paths, which were separated by a single thin bookshelf, but there was no one there.

'Are you invisible?' Ember whispered.

'Oh, I hope so. I've always wanted to see an invisible person!' said Hans, looking around excitedly.

'Invisible? I've never been so insulted in all of my life.'

That was when Ember spotted it.

Peering out from between two books, on a shelf level with Ember's nose, was a tiny creature, about as big as a finger. She moved closer and closer until—

'It's about time you found me. *Invisible*, honestly. Do I look invisible to you?'

He certainly didn't. Ember was speechless. It was undoubtably a worm, a long, thin worm, whose body scrunched together and stretched out as it moved along the shelf to get a better look at her. But it wasn't like the worms she found in the garden. She'd never seen a worm with a monocle and bright pink bow tie before.

Ember opened her mouth to say something, but nothing came out.

Hans, who never seemed to be lost for words, came to the rescue. 'Hello, fine sir. Look at you! You're like a tiny little piece of spaghetti!' He held out his hand. 'I'm Hans, and this is my bestest friend in the whole world, Ember Shadows.'

'What exactly do you expect me to do?' said the worm. 'Shake your hand?'

Hans hastily pulled back his hand. The worm curled the lower half of his body so he was sort of sitting down and then adjusted his monocle with the pointy tip of his tail.

'I've never met a worm before,' said Ember.

'Luckily for you, you still haven't. I'm not a worm, child. I'm a *bookworm*. It's an entirely different thing.' He yawned and covered his mouth with the tip of his tail. 'Don't they teach children anything?'

'Not anything about bookworms, no.'

He sighed. Ember wondered if all bookworms were so rude.

'Child, have you ever seen a worm read a book? Take part in a studious debate? Consume the pages of Weminghay in a single sitting? No. Of course you haven't. Worms simply roll around in the soil and come naively to the surface when they see a bird. Stupid things. On the other hand, we bookworms, here in the Know-It-Hall, are the *singular* most intelligent species in the entire universe.'

He adjusted his bow tie as if to emphasise his point.

'In that case,' said Ember, an idea starting to form in her mind, 'oh all-knowing one, prove it. Show us how clever you are by telling us which way we have to go.'

The bookworm squinted at her with its tiny brown eyes. 'Do you really think I'm going to fall for your childish games?'

It had been worth a try.

'If you want to know the way, you must answer a riddle. Prove *your* knowledge, and I will share mine.'

Hans sprang up and down. 'Oooooh, I love riddles!' he said. 'They always sound so nice, and make you want to dance.'

'No, Hans,' Ember said. 'That's a fiddle.'

The worm rolled its eyes. 'I ought to warn you, there is a forfeit if you answer incorrectly.'

Ember was sure the bookworm's tiny face looked smug. 'What is it?'

'Well, bookworms do of course have the power to turn others into bookworms. How else would we spread the joy of reading and knowledge? And you know, I think you would both make *charming* bookworms.' He leant forward, lips curled in a wry smile. 'Ready?'

Ember tried to hide her shock. She certainly wasn't ready to be turned into a worm! But what choice did she have? She looked down at Hans, who hopping from one foot to the other, seemingly unfazed by the idea of a life spent wriggling around between books.

She nodded at the worm. 'All right.'

The bookworm stretched up to a standing shape, his tail slightly bent to keep himself steady. 'First, tell me. Are you here to fix the mountain?'

'Is this the riddle?' Ember asked, confused.

'No,' the bookworm said, 'it's a matter of personal curiosity.'

'Well . . . no. I'm here to stop my sister from dying, and hopefully get a fate for myself as well.'

His face didn't shift. 'Interesting. You know it would be *rather* quaint if you could help fix the mountain while you're here. It's been awfully quiet this last century. Not much to do since the threads stopped coming through and running around the Know-It-Hall. I almost miss them.'

'I don't have time for that!' cried Ember. 'I need to get going. Please, just give us the riddle.'

He paused and she felt him size her up, before finally

he spoke. '*What belongs to you, but others use it more?*'

Ember hadn't heard that one before. But that didn't matter. She was clever, she could work it out.

Next to her, Hans bounced up and down, his face a picture of concentration. Suddenly, as the answer began to light up in Ember's mind, he erupted.

'SANDWICHES!' he screamed. 'Sandwiches! They belong to you, but you *always* share sandwiches!'

Ember's heart shot up to her throat. 'No! It's not, it's not!' she said, waving her hands at the bookworm. 'That's not our answer!'

'Too late,' said the bookworm. He raised his tail above his head and it began to glow a warm yellow, shaking and shivering as he pointed it at them.

They were going to be turned into wriggling bookworms, trapped in a giant library, and any chance of saving Juniper would be gone!

'Wait!' Ember shouted. 'What if I give you something, and in exchange you give us another try?'

The bookworm paused, his glowing tail hovering in mid-air. His eyes narrowed. 'What sort of thing?'

Ember's hands trembled as she swung her bag round to the front, praying that the bookworm would be as greedy as Flint had been. 'Anything. I can give you a light, a quill that writes on its own, tools—'

'Does your quill have ink?'

Their eyes locked and Ember nodded frantically as she pulled the Auto-Quill Inkorporated out of her bag. 'Yes, look, here, have this.'

'I don't want all that hodgepodge – just the ink.'

Ember grabbed the tiny ink pot and yanked it from the quill, feeling a small tug at her heart as she destroyed her invention. But it was necessary.

The bookworm pushed the pot out of sight between two books. 'Now I can write my own books,' he said, his voice slightly cheerier.

'Second try,' said Hans. He began bobbing up and down again. 'We can do this!'

'No,' snapped Ember, more harshly than she'd meant to. 'Look, Hans, leave the riddle to me, OK?'

'But it's my job to help you!'

'Hans, it's really important that we get this right, and quickly. Please, be quiet!' She didn't think the bookworm would let them trade their way out of being turned into bookworms if they answered wrong a second time.

Hans' face dropped. But it was for the best.

She'd nearly had the answer before. *What belongs to you, but others use it more?* Ember tried to ignore Hans. He looked so glum and worried, more anxious even than when he'd found the book with his name on—

'That's it!' she shouted. 'Your *name*. It belongs to you, but other people use it more, when they say it.'

Ember turned to tell Hans how she had worked it out, how he had helped her even without saying a word, when the floor began to shudder and shake. Hans jumped up and clung to her and she pulled him close. She reached out and grabbed hold of the shelf but it was juddering too, shaking and vibrating like the whole realm had been hit by an earthquake.

'What's happening?' she called, but the bookworm had disappeared.

The shelf pulled away from her grip and started to move towards the right side of the fork. In a moment it had closed off the right-hand path, until there was only one road ahead of them. Then, as quickly as the shaking had begun, it stopped.

She looked again for the smug bookworm, but as

she scanned the shelves for him, she spotted a different animal.

Another origami bird. Perched on a shelf ahead of them, the bird was staring straight at her.

It must have been watching her the whole time.

*

It wasn't long until Ember, trailed by Hans who insisted on walking behind so he didn't 'get in the way', reached another fork in the path, where another bookworm was busy reading, sat on the pages of an open book.

This second bookworm was wearing a huge pair of glasses, even though he had no ears or nose to keep them on. Rather than a pink bow tie, he wore a tiny knitted vest.

'Excuse me,' said Ember politely. 'Might you be able to tell us which way to go?'

He groaned loudly.

'Or could you at least give us a riddle?' asked Ember.

'I have so many better things to be doing,' the bookworm said with a yawn. 'But fine. Ready? *The more there is, the less you see.* What is it?'

She knew that one instantly. 'Darkness!' she said. 'The more darkness there is, the less you can see.'

'I don't need you to explain it to me,' he said, rolling his eyes and returning to his reading, as the world around them shuddered and shook.

Ember held out her arms for Hans to jump up, but he remained on the ground, the vibration of the shelves making him shake like a leaf.

'Hans, I didn't mean to upset you,' she said. 'I need to make sure we get these right, that's all.'

He nodded but continued on the new path without even looking at her. Great. A sulky Hans was even worse than a happy one.

They walked in silence. Ember looked out for any books about clocks, but she didn't point out the incredible bookbirds, or the bright colours of the spines, or the thousands of tiny bookworms she had spotted, each one dressed differently to the next. Hans' silence took all the fun out of it. Not to mention the fact he was much slower when sulking, and the ticking of Juniper's clock felt like it was drumming through her bag and right into her body. They didn't have time to waste on arguing.

It was almost a relief to reach a dead end and find another bookworm waiting. This one had long brown hair piled on top of her head in a little bun and wore a purple dress that stretched down about a third of her body before flaring out. Her tail-end stuck out at the bottom and she was using it to tidy books on the shelf.

Hans sat on the floor and leant against the bookcase, arms crossed. Ember rolled her eyes. She'd apologise again once she'd figured out the next riddle. He didn't need to be such a baby about it.

'Hello,' she said. 'Could we have the riddle, please?'

'It's the last one, so make sure you're ready,' the bookworm said, not even bothering to face Ember.

'Last one?' Ember bit her lip. She'd hoped they would have come across a book that might have helped them fix Juniper's clock. But at least they were on their way – somewhere.

'I'm ready,' she said.

'*Until I am measured, I am not known. But you will miss me once I have flown.* What am I?'

The bookworm stared expectantly at her. But Ember's mind was blank.

She was stumped.

12

No matter how many times she paced between the shelves, no matter how many times she racked her brain, Ember simply didn't know the answer to the bookworm's riddle.

'*Until I am measured, I am not known. But you will miss me once I have flown,*' she muttered.

'You know,' droned the bookworm, 'if you don't answer you'll be stuck here for ever.'

This information was about as helpful as Hans, who was now lying on the floor, arms spread wide, sighing every now and then.

'Give me a moment,' Ember said. She could get this. She looked around at the shelves for inspiration.

Wait, was that . . .

A triangle of grey poked out from the side of the bookshelves. It was someone's elbow, and she knew exactly whose.

'You! What are you doing here?'

Flint crept sheepishly out from behind the shelves where he'd been hiding. He was still wearing the Shh!-Oos – *her* Shh!-Oos. 'Come to check you haven't ruined everything yet,' he said.

'Flint!' shouted Hans, bouncing up to him, no longer in a sulk.

'You know each other?' asked Ember.

'Flint came through the Forest of Time years and years ago,' Hans explained to Ember. 'He had run away from the village because he was too scared to get some funny card in the post or something and he—'

'All right, thanks Hans!' Flint said, cutting him off. His cheeks had turned red.

'No, Hans, carry on,' said Ember.

Hans looked back and forth between Ember and Flint. She could tell that he was torn between loyalty to Ember, his new best friend, and the fact he was meant to be annoyed at her.

Finally, he burst out, 'He was too scared to get a card in the post so came to the mountain to hide!'

Something clicked into place in Ember's mind. 'So you're the boy!'

Flint shuffled his feet. 'None o' your business.'

'You are! The boy Ms Daylands said went missing! But . . . I thought they found an oar, and your note said you'd gone to another village.'

'Well I'm not an idiot, am I? Had to lead them off on the wrong path. No one ever thought I'd be up here, did they?'

'But your family . . .' said Ember. How could he have left them?

Flint looked down. 'Yeah,' he said. 'I know. I miss Ma and Pa a lot.'

'Then why don't you go home?'

'It's too late, ain't it? Once you step on the mountain . . .'

'. . . you lose your fate.' Ember felt something tug in her chest; she knew how it felt not to have a fate.

Still, it wasn't right. His parents had no idea he was still alive and here he was, right in front of her. She wanted to do something, to say something.

But the ticking of Juniper's clock in her bag stopped her. She had her own family to worry about.

'Anyway,' Flint said. 'I actually came to tell you to give up climbing the mountain – it's too dangerous! Come and live at the bottom with me instead, you can do whatever you want.'

Sadness swept over Ember as she realised how similar she and Flint truly were. He had run away at her age all those years ago because he was scared of the future. She was scared of the future too, but there was one difference between them.

'I can't. I have to save my sister,' she said.

'What makes you think you can? You're only a kid.'

'I have to try.'

'Not true. You can give up and admit you're scared. Sometimes you've got to listen to that fear! It's much easier to listen to that fear than all those silly other thoughts.'

121

Flint was wrong. He had to be wrong. If Ember listened to all the fears slithering through her mind, she'd give up like he had done. And then what would that mean for Juniper?

No. Ember had something to fight for; she had made a promise.

'Are you going to take much longer?' The bookworm's voice broke through her thoughts. 'I'll say it once more for you, and then your time's up. I have better things to do than listen to this squabbling all day.' She cleared her throat. '*Until I am measured, I am not known. But you will miss me once I have flown. What am I?*'

'I know the answer!' shouted Hans suddenly.

'No, Hans, please be quiet, I'm trying to think!'

'Do you know something, Ember Shadows?' he said. His arms were folded across his tiny chest as he faced her. 'You're not very clever.'

'That's not going to help us here, Hans.'

'Then you should give up. Because you don't know anything. Nothing. You're just – just – just hot little bits of fire, making a fuss!'

Even his insults didn't make sense, Ember thought.

She started pacing again, ignoring both Hans and Flint. She knew she was smart, and she *would* get it, she'd be able to get it. She had to. Juniper's life depended on it.

'Maybe it's a flamingo?' she muttered to herself.

The bookworm let out a sarcastic laugh. 'I'll assume that wasn't your answer.'

'That's it. Last chance!' said Flint, turning to leave. 'I ain't getting stuck here again.'

'We're not leaving,' she said.

'Suit yourself.' Flint walked off, back the way they had come, leaving her with a very grumpy Hans.

He leant against the shelf, under the worm, and Ember noticed with a jolt of fear that five white paper birds were perched next to him. 'You're the most unclever person I've ever met,' said Hans.

She could feel rage boiling in her stomach. Panic was setting in. She had to get this right or they'd be stuck in between these shelves until, well, she didn't know when, and all Hans was doing was making things harder.

'For goodness' sake, I'm trying to fix this!' she cried.

'Fix what?'

'You wouldn't understand.'

'Understand what?'

'Everything!' she snapped. Her anger boiled over and tumbled out. 'All of this. Don't you get it? I have to get this right. If I don't, I'll be stuck, and Juniper will die in less than three hours! And I'll be left with some empty Fate Card that means nothing. There will be no point to any of this. I'll never make a difference, I'll never change anything or invent something new, I'll never save Juniper and my dad will have died for nothing. He'll have saved my life, only for me to get trapped in a bunch of bookcases, living some empty life without a destiny and letting Juniper die before she even hits her ninth birthday. I'm running out of time!'

She stood, her heart burning as it raced against her ribs. Hans stared up at her with his bright unblinking eyes. 'That's the answer,' he whispered.

'What?'

Just then, one of the white birds swooped down between them and hit the floor with a slap. The origami shape spun vigorously in front of them and, as Ember crouched down, the body parts began to unfold.

The bird opened completely to form a piece of white card, with one word written on it: *Time*.

It was a Fate Card, Ember realised. But where the name would have been printed on a normal Fate Card, two black raven eyes stared back, the word written below them like a mouth.

'It's the answer to the riddle.' Hans tried to smile. 'Time.'

He was right. The birds had given her the answer, too. But they were omens, everyone knew that. Why would they be trying to help her? It didn't make sense.

Ember reached out to touch the card, but, just like the birds back in Everspring had done, it burst into flames, leaving a pile of fizzing embers on the floor between them.

A moment later, the shaking began again and everything hummed and thundered beneath their feet. The bookshelf that had been blocking their way split in two, right down the middle, sending frightened books into the air to find another shelf, as a door-sized gap opened up.

'You are now leaving the Know-It-Hall,' groaned the bookworm, who had been knocked to the floor by the realm-quake and was left staring miserably up at the shelves she needed to scale. 'Please, don't come back.'

13

Blinding white light forced Ember to screw up her eyes as they entered the next realm. To her relief it dimmed, but then, before her eyes had adjusted, the light faded to pitch black.

Everywhere she looked was dark as night, as though she still had her eyes closed. She couldn't make out the sky any more, or whether they were even outside.

'Where are we?' asked Hans.

'I don't know. And that bird – where did it come from?'

'I don't know.' He kicked the ground. 'Didn't need it anyway. I knew the answer.'

She reached into her bag and fumbled around for the Nothing-Goes-Bump-In-The-Light. Once she shook it and the air was filled with light from the luminescent plants, she grabbed Juniper's clock.

02:01.

'Hans, we've lost nearly a whole hour already!'

'We have?'

'Look!' She held the jar over the clock as another minute vanished from their countdown. 'Two hours left. What are we going to do?'

'It's like the riddle – time has flown,' said Hans, his frustration disappearing as he made a joke. 'Ha!'

But a glare from Ember silenced him. This wasn't funny. Apart from the small circle of light from her jar, they were wrapped in complete darkness, alone, and without any way of knowing where to go next.

'How has time gone so quickly?' she muttered.

She held the light out in front of her to try and figure out which way to go but there was no path. She would have to make a decision and hope for the best.

'Come on, Hans. This way.'

As Ember grabbed his hand, a deafening *POP* broke through the dark, as loud as thunder. With it, a thin ray of light appeared from above and illuminated something ahead of them. Was that . . .? Surely it couldn't be a train?

It was. The train had a shiny little blue-and-white striped engine at the front, which puffed out grey steam, and four gleaming matching carriages trailing behind.

Each carriage had plush blue seats, and looked big enough for two people.

'Wow,' whispered Hans. 'Is that a boat?'

'It's a *train*. Look, you can see the engine.'

The pair of them walked up to the front, where they found something stranger still.

In the engine carriage, slumped over a desk of levers and buttons and pulleys, was a woman with dark brown hair as smooth as melted chocolate. Hans went towards her.

'She's sleeping!' he mouthed, putting a tiny finger to his lips.

Ember crept closer. The woman was wearing a blue trouser suit, with stripes that matched the train. On her head was a white hat, round on the top with a visor sticking out of the front. Ember tiptoed closer behind Hans. Silver lettering had been stitched along the top of the hat. *Conductor*.

'*AHHHHHH!!!!!!!!!!!!!*' The woman shrieked, sat up like a bolt of lightning and smacked her head against the train.

'AHHHHHHHHHH!!' Hans and Ember's squeals blended into a single high-pitched scream as Hans leapt into Ember's arms.

The woman scrambled out of the train and stood up, adjusting her hat. All three of them looked at each other, eyes flitting from one shocked face to the next.

'Ember Shadows!' Suddenly, the woman broke into a smile. 'You're here! Oh, I'm so sorry about all of that. Sleeping on the job – don't tell my manager now, will you?' She winked at Ember, who must have looked as confused as she felt, because the woman leant forward and whispered, 'Just kidding.'

But Ember didn't feel like laughing. There was a knot growing in her throat. The woman was acting as though she, Ember, was famous. So had Hans, when he'd met her. But something felt off about it this time, like she'd taken a bite of a biscuit and found it was salty rather than sweet.

'How do you know my name?' she asked.

'Lucky guess,' the woman said, with a bright, white, toothy smile. 'Anyway,' she carried on. 'I am so pleased to meet you, what a real pleasure. Haven't seen anyone up here in a long time now. Just been little old me.' She fiddled with her hair, brushed it down over her shoulders and straightened her blue and white blazer over her white shirt. On the lapel, she wore a black pin badge, with a silver jagged line crossing from one side to the other, and four tiny letters: N, E, S and W bordering the circular shape as they would points on a compass.

'My name is Moira,' the woman continued. 'And I'm here to welcome you to our tour today!'

The woman had huge eyes and long lashes that fluttered up and down again and again as she spoke. Everything about her seemed doll-like: the stiff way she stood, the flat material of her suit, her over-shiny hair. She didn't seem like a normal person, at least not like the people Ember had met. Maybe she was nervous as she hadn't spoken to anyone in a long time. Ember edged forward slightly to get a better look. Moira simply smiled, a row of perfectly white teeth on display.

'Sorry,' said Ember. 'What tour?'

'Why, your tour of the Messy Middle of course! I'm Tour Manager and,' she leant forward, 'General Manager too, in my opinion, of this charming realm. Although I really do think we ought to give it a new name these days. Maybe we should call it the *Not-So*-Messy Middle. What do you say?' She winked again at Ember.

'I guess,' Ember said uncertainly. She looked at Hans, who shrugged back at her. Things must have got weird if they were strange even by his standards.

'Well, then, what are we waiting for? Let's hop aboard and find out what's in store!' Moira climbed back into the engine carriage, pushed a few buttons, and a fanfare noise ripped through the air.

'Um, no thanks,' said Ember, though Hans was looking intrigued now. 'We don't have time. I have to find something that can help my sister, and—'

'Can you keep a secret?' whispered Moira. Her eyes were wide as she stared at Ember. There was definitely something strange about her face, as though it had been pulled into a smile and frozen there.

Ember nodded.

'I think you're closer to helping your sister than you realise. You need to keep going.' Moira patted the seat next to her. 'Tell you what, I'll give you the VIP treatment. You two can sit up front!'

Ember looked around for other options. She needed to find something that would fix Juniper's clock, but with darkness as far as she could see in every direction, she didn't seem to have any other choice.

Moira was looking at her expectantly, as though she had been waiting for this day for years. Maybe she had. With no alternative, Ember sighed and took the space next to Moira, while Hans squeezed on to the seat next to her. Bag firmly between her feet, she was ready. For what, she wasn't sure.

When they were settled, Moira picked up a microphone and spoke into it, as if she were talking to a whole crowd of people. 'Welcome aboard, esteemed guests. It is mighty fine to have you here in the Messy Middle!'

Hans leant over to Ember. 'Did you hear that? Steamed! I don't think I've ever been a steamed guest!'

Moira carried on.

'Today we'll be taking a trip down Memory-To-Be-Lane. As you probably already know, the Messy Middle is a realm where we show you what lies ahead, everything that will make you *you*. You'll find your purpose, your hobbies and you'll even get a sneak peek at the lucky love of your life! Let's hope they're dreamy, am I right?'

'Yes! *Super* dreamy,' said Hans, clapping his hands together.

'Yuck,' whispered Ember.

But even as she said it, something inside her flickered. Did this mean she was finally going to find out what fate had in store for her? Was this realm a way to see everything that her Fate Card had failed to show?

'You'll be seeing all of this as snapshots, pictures, photos, freeze-frames – whatever you'd like to call them. Imagine the Messy Middle as the photo album of your life to come! We use giant snow globes to show you all of these wonderful moments, so sadly you can't get up close and personal today. But don't worry, one day soon you'll be living these freeze-frames yourself!'

She clearly knew the speech word for word, thought Ember.

'Now for those safety requirements. The ride isn't as bumpy as it used to be, thank goodness! But please remember to keep all hands and feet inside the carriage at all times. And remember, it's your life! So, let's have a little fun, shall we?'

With one final wink, Moira placed the microphone in a holder next to the control panel. Her hands moved so fast they seemed to blur, as she twisted knobs, jabbed some buttons and then –

The train came to life and began chugging away. They were off.

One by one, lights came on around them, and Ember could make out a track ahead. This was it. The Messy Middle of her life, revealed. She was finally going to have her whole life mapped out for her! Despite her worry about Juniper, a thread of excitement snaked through her. After all this time, she was going to find out what her future held. She screwed her eyes closed and made a silent wish: *Let Juniper grow old and let*

me be an inventor. Then she opened her eyes and crossed her fingers, hoping.

Ahead of them, an arch popped up from nowhere, like the one she had come through at the bottom of the mountain. Only woven into the iron pattern of *this* one was her own name. On top, two paper birds stared down at them. As they passed underneath a cold shiver crept over her skin.

'We are now entering the Messy Middle of Ember Shadows,' said Moira. She turned and beamed her trademark smile. 'Great name, by the way!'

Ahead, there was nothing.

Ember winced and her flicker of hope was extinguished in one quick puff. Of course there was nothing in her future; the cards had already told her that.

A click sounded somewhere above them, followed by a short hiss of static, and then an upbeat piano song began to play. A second later and to her right, a light came on, revealing a huge freeze-frame.

Moira was right; it looked like an enormous snow globe. It was illuminated from above and within the giant dome was a roundhouse, with bright yellow walls and a thatched roof. In front stood the most peculiar thing: a perfect copy of Ember, frozen, as though time had stopped her mid-action.

Except, she looked taller than the real Ember. And older, much older. She was maybe twenty-something and her hair had been chopped off around the shoulders, but it was definitely her. Her hand was outstretched in a wave as though she'd seen someone she knew.

'My, my, we've come to the first snapshot of your Messy Middle, Ember Shadows. Here you can see your wonderful home!'

Ember's stomach started to flutter again. She had a future, she really did! The house looked so tidy, so beautiful, everything about it was amazing. And future-Ember looked happy. Relief washed over her. It might only be a house, but it was already so much more than the card had revealed.

'Wow! Yellow! That's my new favourite colour,' shouted Hans.

The train slowed down a fraction for them to take a longer look. The garden surrounding the house was filled with yellow daffodils, and in the windows there were blue curtains. Ember wanted to remember every inch of it – the dark trousers and red top she was wearing, the pattern of flowers painted on the front door – but the train started to speed up again and they were off.

As the light faded over the globe, Ember craned her neck to look back for a final glimpse, and she could have sworn the walls of the house had changed colour. No. She was imagining it; they couldn't be green. She turned further to get a better look but it had been plunged into darkness. The music carried on as the train sped up and another light flickered on, this time on Moira's side of the train.

'My, my, what a great life you're having so far, Ember! Here we've got your favourite hobbies. Look! There's baking-Ember making some dragonflutter cakes, and bungee-ball-Ember, and even swimming-Ember! Super talented, and I can't say I'm surprised,' called Moira's honey voice.

Ember studied the three perfect models of herself frozen in the snow globe. One of them was mixing something in a bowl, her tongue sticking out as she concentrated. Another was celebrating with her leg right up in the air after a huge kick, the tiny glowing ball on a long elastic shooting out from her foot, and the last one was sitting on the bank of an immense river – it must have been Border River – smiling and dripping wet in a swimsuit.

'But that can't be right,' Ember said. 'I hate water . . .'

'Look,' said Hans. 'It's moving.'

The Ember by the river had twitched. Just a finger. But then her elbows jerked, her neck swivelled, and suddenly the whole of the model went fuzzy. A second later, model-Ember was standing up, wearing a dress, and frowning down at a book, as if she were lost in a story.

'My, my,' said Moira. Frantically, she started pushing buttons. 'I – well, this isn't meant to happen, folks. Please, hold on one moment.'

The three future-Embers plunged into darkness and the train sped up.

'Seem to be having a little malfunction over there, but not to worry, on to the next stop!' Moira's voice was faltering. Ember could tell something was wrong. But the train kept going, the music playing the same tune over and over.

The third snow globe was on Hans' side.

'Here we are,' said Moira. 'This seems to be back to normal now, and what have we here? Ooooh, *relationships!*' She turned and grinned, winking *again*.

Ember blushed. She stared at the freeze-frame where model-Ember was standing, hands outstretched and leaning forward. Leaning towards her, clasping her hands, was a boy. And that wasn't the worst part. He was leaning in to *kiss* her.

'Wow, he really is dreamy!' said Hans. 'What a dreamy dream.'

The boy had blond hair and freckles. He wasn't exactly ugly, thought Ember, but still . . . 'Can we go to the next one?' she said. 'I don't really want to . . .' But she trailed off.

Something strange was happening.

The image glitched.

The boy she'd seen seconds ago had been replaced. The new one had smooth, dark copper skin, black hair, and he was tall. Model-Ember was having to reach up to him.

It glitched again.

This time it was a girl. She was beautiful, with long red hair straight as could be.

Then it was a boy again. Then it was a group of friends all around Ember, dancing. Then it was Ember alone, smiling into the distance. Ember lost track as it sped through options, people appearing and disappearing in seconds.

'What's going on?' called Ember. The music grew louder. The train lurched forward and the light above kissing-Ember went out, then came back on. Ember turned back to watch as it kept switching on and off, a different freeze-frame revealed each time.

'Oh my gosh,' said Moira. 'I should have known . . .' She started pressing buttons again, trying to control the juddering train.

'Moira, what's happening?' Ember called. Something was very wrong.

Another snow globe next to Hans lit up. A smiling model-Ember beamed at them, holding a screwdriver. Then the screwdriver became a loaf of bread, then a quill, then it was a paintbrush. And there, perched on the easel next to future-Ember, was another origami bird.

Moira grabbed the side of the train. Her picture-perfect smile had disappeared, and mania had taken over. 'This hasn't happened for years! No, no, no!'

The lurching was getting worse and Hans was flying around everywhere. Ember grabbed him, pushed him inside her jacket and zipped it up.

'It's the Messy Middle again! Every fate in here should be fixed, it should be decided. But yours, yours is still so messy! I suppose I shouldn't be surprised, but really – *this* messy?'

Moira pulled levers and flicked switches, but nothing changed. The train hurtled forward and backwards, tipped on to its side and back upright.

Then, it came to a halt. Everything went very still.

The piano music stopped.

It was silent. Only the flashing lights continued, illuminating the terrifying snow globes with thousands of different Embers all around them.

'Moira, we don't have time for this!' Ember pulled the clock from her bag as the lights flashed and Moira hit buttons.

1:20. But that couldn't be right! They had only just got here. How had so much time vanished so quickly?

'This is the problem with these messy fates,' muttered Moira. 'You remember that. Nothing works properly unless you have things balanced.'

'Moira, we have to get a move on!' Ember only had an hour and twenty minutes to save her sister. She couldn't spend that time stuck on a train!

Ember pushed the clock in her pocket and desperately searched the control panel herself for something helpful. Everything was mixed up – speed dials and engine starters, buttons as big as her head, tiny pinprick switches, all of them with strange words and nonsense meanings. *Supersonic. Freeze-me. Simple Life. Slow-me-down. Smooth Sailing.* Then, she spotted one that might help.

Get-me-outta-here-quick!

She reached for the button without thinking twice, and her fingers met the bright orange circle. Moira shouted. 'No!'

But she was too late.

The train juddered. Moira pulled a long metal safety bar over their heads, crossed her fingers, and closed her eyes.

'What now?' whispered Hans, his face peeking out of Ember's jacket.

'You should probably hold on,' said Moira. 'Hold on *tight*.'

14

The train started again.

It began slowly, a loud clunk coming from beneath them every few seconds as the train sped up. And then, Ember felt the angle of the train change. They were going up. They went higher and higher and higher and the track got steeper and steeper and steeper until Ember's back was digging into the seat with the force of gravity, and the safety bar was gripping at her waist. From beneath, she could hear the *clank, clank, clank* as the wheels clung to the track.

She dared herself to look back and immediately regretted it. Behind her, the carriages hung out like a tail, a long snaking shape dangling down to the earth. They were so high up, the snow globes seemed like puddles below them.

The engine slowed to a stop.

They were hanging, completely vertical, stuck in the air. Ember swallowed. Something told her exactly what was coming next, and it was not going to be good. The train inched forward, crawling up centimetre by centimetre until, slowly, it flattened out again. They had reached the tipping point. They were going over. They were going to . . .

'AHHHHHHHHHHHHHHHHHHHHHHHHHHH-HHHHHHHHHHHHHHHHHH!'

They plummeted down, down, right down, twisting, turning, shaking over the track as it weaved like a dragon through the night. Ember's heart hammered in her ears. Her stomach and brain had gone into shock without gravity and every organ felt like it was rattling around inside her, desperate for the train to stop. Flashes of light blinded her as they snaked up and down at breakneck speed and someone's screams were filling her ears – her own? She couldn't tell any more. The train kept going, racing round and round the track. They could barely see more than five metres ahead, so there was no way of knowing where it would go next, if it would stop, where it would take them.

'Moira!' she screamed. 'Can't you stop it?'

'It's the rollercoaster of life Ember, you can't stop it once you're halfway through!'

'Wooooooooo-eeeeeee!' Hans called out from the safety of her jacket. 'We're flying!'

Ember's hands gripped the safety bar, and she squeezed her eyes closed. Every second she was tossed one way, then back, but to her relief she felt the train slowing slightly. But then they tilted, and the train was climbing again, higher and higher, until it came to an unnerving stop. Her hair was swishing around her, hanging into the empty air *above* her head.

Did that mean . . .? She tore one eyelid open and instantly wished she hadn't.

They were completely upside-down! Far below them were the snow globes, like distant stars in the darkness. She prised one hand from the safety bar and clamped it over her pocket – she couldn't let Juniper's clock fall!

'Ahhhh!' she screamed. 'Moira, we're stuck!'

Moira twisted around so her face was inches away from Ember's, and Ember saw with a start that her eyes were now red around the edges. Something had snapped in her, and the strange happy personality had shifted.

She was furious.

'This is all your fault!' she snarled. 'There's nothing I can do now, Ember. That's why they call it the Messy Middle!'

'But what happens next?'

'That's the horror of it all, we don't know! This is exactly the problem with fates!'

Ember felt Hans' hands cling tightly to her shirt and the train started to clank forward slowly, until . . .

Whooosh! They were off again, hurtling through the dark, juddering from side to side. She didn't dare open her eyes again until finally, the train started to slow down. This time Ember could feel they were the right way up. The darkness softened and Ember opened her eyes. They had arrived back on the ground.

'Well, *esteemed* guests,' Moira said, sarcasm dripping from her voice, 'we have reached the end of the Messy Middle. And my, my, what a messy one that was.'

She glared at Ember as the train tremored to a stop and the safety bar rose from their laps. Hans pulled himself out of Ember's jacket and jumped on to the seat next to her.

'Let's do it again!' he said, clapping his hands together.

'No. Never again,' said Ember. She clambered out of the train as quickly as she could. Her legs were like jelly. Every single part of her body tingled. Even her hair felt like it had been electrocuted.

It was dark again, but along with their own spotlight, another was shining over a single door, metres away from where the track came to an end.

'Thank you so much for riding through the Messy Middle today,' said Moira from the engine cart, although she certainly didn't sound very thankful. 'We really appreciate you choosing us as your mode of transport through some of the highlights of your life. I'd like to personally wish you a fabulous onward journey!'

'Wait, Moira,' Ember said. 'What was all of that? Why did it—' But before she could say any more, Moira and the train disappeared with a *POP*, leaving behind nothing but a cloud of grey steam. She turned to Hans. 'I don't think she liked my middle, do you?'

Hans shook his head. 'Now what? How much time do we have left?'

Ember pulled out Juniper's clock, but as she turned it over, her stomach sank. A great big crack had formed down the middle; the glass had completely split in two. She traced over it with her fingers.

'How did this happen?' she said, falling to her knees.

But she knew. She knew that it was her fault. She'd been so desperate to get off the train and get on with their task, that she had pushed that *Get-me-outta-here-quick* button

without even thinking. The metal safety bar must have hit the clock face while it was in her pocket.

'It's OK, Ember. We'll fix it.'

Ember closed her eyes. It wasn't OK at all. She had broken the clock – again – and was even further away from helping Juniper. It felt as though every step she made on this mountain made things worse.

Eventually, she found the courage to wipe her eyes and peer at the clock's casing.

0:59

'This is hopeless,' she mumbled.

'Definitely,' said Hans. 'You should give up, like Flint said.'

She turned to face him where he stood, arms folded, with one eyebrow raised.

'We can't give up. Juniper needs me,' she whispered.

'EXACTLY!' screamed Hans as he leapt into the air, doing another loop-the-loop. 'So let's go, go, go!'

Ember wished she had a few more minutes to consider what had just happened – the horrible ride, the glitching snow globes, her ever-changing future. Why was her middle so messy when everyone else's was fixed? It didn't seem fair.

But they didn't have time to waste on sulking. Juniper had less than an hour left to live. And that was all that mattered.

'Come on, then,' Ember said. 'Through that door I suppose.' She nodded to the door, which was lit by a spotlight.

'A door! I've never seen a door before. This is really so exciting.'

Blinking back tears, Ember stood up and stepped forward towards the huge charcoal-coloured metal door. Engraved into the metal was an intricate pattern of tiny leaves and vines, each one twirling in on itself, spreading from the corners of the door all the way to the centre, where they joined together to make three words.

'*Garden of Gifts*,' read Hans, sounding the words out carefully. 'What are *gifts*?'

'Gifts are things you get given. Like presents.'

'We get a present? I want a dog! No, a hippo! No, I want a set of ears, definitely ears.' He cupped his hands to the sides of his face, making pretend ears. 'Think about how much I'd be able to hear then!'

As awful as the weight of Juniper's clock felt in her pocket, Ember managed a smile. It wasn't going to be as simple as walking in and getting a present, she was sure about that, but Hans' optimism gave her the strength she needed to take the final step forward to the door.

She gripped the cold, rounded door handle, and

pulled. When nothing happened, Hans joined in with his tiny hands, and the pair heaved and heaved until, finally, the door banged open and revealed the Garden of Gifts.

15

Sunshine flooded the blossoming realm ahead of them. The garden was beyond anything Ember had seen in the village. It was packed with flourishing flowerbeds and exotic plants, and the walls surrounding it were covered in tangled ivy climbing up towards the bright sky above. Everywhere Ember looked, colour burst from buds and shrubs. A path in front of them led between the flowerbeds to a circular pool of coloured water, and on either side of the pool were two marble fountains, each topped with a statue of a person.

Behind the two statues was a sight that stopped Ember in her tracks. A rainbow waterfall crashed down the back wall, splashing into the pool beneath. The colour of the water changed as it flowed – red, purple, gold, peach and, she could have sworn, the exact shade of green covering her bedroom walls. It was magnificent beyond anything she could have imagined.

'Should we talk to her?' said Hans, pointing to one of the statues. 'She looks like a brainy brain.'

'She's a *statue*, Hans,' Ember said.

'And I'm a clock hand.'

He made a good point. And the statue was right in front of the shimmering waterfall, which looked like the most magical part of the garden. So she nodded, and they hurried along the path, between two flowerbeds filled with tulips. As they rushed past, thousands of petals leapt from their flowers and darted into the air. Like a flutter of butterflies, they flew towards the ivy-covered walls where they resettled, reforming their flower shapes. Ember shook her head and carried on; there was no time to be distracted.

As they approached the pool, Ember realised that on either side of the crashing waterfall, clinging to the rock wall, were hundreds of glass jars and containers of different shapes and sizes. The containers were leaping from their places on the wall and flying through the air. Ember watched as a tall purple bottle jumped from the rock and positioned itself above the crashing water. Its cork stopper popped from the top and hung in mid-air as the bottle poured its glittering liquid into the waterfall. Once the bottle had emptied, the stopper hopped back into the top, and then the bottle magically refilled with the same purple liquid, before flying back to its place on the wall.

Hans trotted towards the fountain on the left side of the pool, where the marble statue of a woman stood proudly over the jets of water. She was holding a book and her shoulders were back, her face a picture of concentration as water erupted from the pool around her skirt. She looked like the kind of person who should be running the world, like she would know exactly what to do in any situation – even Ember's. The fountain on the right side of the pool was topped with a man, one hand stretched up to the sky, the other holding a long, thin, brass telescope.

'I think he's an astronomer,' said Hans.

'You haven't ever seen a door, but you know what an astronomer is?' asked Ember.

Hans shrugged. 'Well, aren't you going to ask them for help?'

'I guess,' said Ember. Now they were closer, it seemed even more ridiculous; there was no sign of life from the marble forms.

But they still hadn't found a spare part for Juniper's clock, and there was no one else to ask for help. Ember held her hand out and touched the marble base. 'Excuse me,' she said, feeling very silly. 'Can you help us?'

Nothing happened. The garden was still, except for the crashing waves of the waterfall.

'See?' Ember said. 'Told you it was just a—'

But before she could finish her sentence, the stone started to shake, sending ripples through the fountain's water. She glanced across at the man – he was shaking, too. Both of them began to crack, tiny canyons forming all over their bodies until the stone shifted, and suddenly a layer of it shed like a snakeskin. Beneath, the two figures were still made of smooth marble, but now they seemed *very* much alive, and they were looking right at her.

'A statue?' said the woman, snapping her book closed. 'I wouldn't say I was a statue.'

'Nor me,' said the man. 'Far from it. I'm an astronomer.'

The man twirled his telescope between his fingers, as he narrowed his eyes at Ember. 'What are you?' he said.

The woman peered down. 'Yes, what are you?'

'I'm Hans!' shouted Hans. 'I'm a spare part, which I think is a tragedy, such a tragedy, because—'

'No,' said the woman, staring at Ember as though she wanted to see right inside her. '*You*. What are you?'

Ember opened her mouth to

speak, but what could she say? She couldn't exactly say she was an engineer or an inventor. She was only a child and according to her Fate Card she wasn't ever going to be anything.

'I'm . . . Ember,' she said finally.

'That's *who*, not what,' said the man. He put his hands on his hips. 'I think I'll be a doctor now.' He clicked his fingers and the brass telescope disappeared with a *pop*. Now, around his neck was a stethoscope, dangling down over a doctor's lab coat.

'Oh, yes,' said the woman, grinning back at him. 'Good idea.' And with a *snap*, a stethoscope appeared around her neck, too.

'Wow! Then I think I'll be a horse,' said Hans.

The woman smiled down at Hans, and then looked at Ember. 'Have you thought about what you might do with your life, Ember?'

The truth was, for a long time she had thought of nothing else. Ember had spent years dreaming of ways to improve the village. She'd spent most of her life inventing things to help other people, hoping that one day her Fate Card would arrive with that special word, *inventor*. She'd imagined that feeling of finally making it, of finally being who she wanted to be, for years.

But there was no time for that now.

'I'm not here about me. Not any more, anyway. I have to save my sister.'

'This is the Garden of Gifts, you know.' The man played with his stethoscope as he spoke, barely even looking at them. 'Not the Garden of Sister Saving.'

'But maybe one of the gifts can help me save Juniper?' Ember suggested, thinking of the broken clock. 'Do you have any magical glue or . . .' She trailed off as the woman statue began to laugh.

'Oh silly, the gifts aren't that sort of gift,' said the woman. 'They're gifts that you find in yourself, the things you are particularly fantastic at. I suppose you'd call them talents.'

'Well, can one of your *talents* help me?' Ember said, trying not to sound as impatient as she felt.

'That all depends,' said the woman. 'You see, we don't dish out talents willy-nilly! Talents are what make up the very fabric of a person. A little bit of this, a little bit of that, that's the part that puts the *you*, in you!'

'Quite.' The man dropped the stethoscope and turned to the waterfall. 'Some of these talents will already be inside of you, a few of them you'll master later in life, and many of them will *never* be yours.'

At that, he held his hands in the air, wiggled his fingers, and then pointed to a jar. It leapt off the wall and hovered, bright turquoise liquid sloshing around inside. The man flicked his finger towards the waterfall and the jar un-stoppered itself and tipped some of its potion into the cascading water.

'A little bit of Caring Cocktail,' said the man, 'a splash of Precision Pop, and a whole serving of Creature Compound . . .'

Ember watched in fascination as two more jars sprang from the wall and added their magical mixture, turning the waterfall a fabulous shade of watermelon green. The woman clicked her fingers, and suddenly she was dressed in a vet's uniform of the same colour, with a bright orange parrot resting on her shoulder.

'. . . and you've got yourself a vet!' she shouted. 'My turn!'

She turned to the waterfall, waved her hands as the man had done, and bottles began to spring from their places on the wall. 'How about some Justice Jelly and some Feisty Fighting Fluid, not to mention Honourable

Ointment. A splash of Leader Elixir. And *bam*! You've got a . . .'

'Council Leader!' the man shouted. He snapped his fingers and he was dressed like Ms Daylands, complete with a long, ruby-red cloak.

'Wow! What else can you be?' said Hans.

But Ember cut in before they started again. 'I need some help fixing a clock, so how about becoming a clockmaker?'

'Ooh, no sorry, I don't want to be a clockmaker today.' Another click of the fingers and the woman was surrounded by tiny stone books. 'I'd rather be a writer.'

'Yes, me too,' said the man, switching out his own Council Leader's cloak for a parchment and quill.

'But surely you could—'

'No,' they said in unison.

'I only need you to—'

'No.'

Ember glared up at them. They were being intentionally difficult.

'I have an idea,' said the marble man. 'How about *you* become the clockmaker, Ember?'

'What a wonderful idea!' The woman clapped her hands together.

'I can't just become a clockmaker,' Ember said. 'It doesn't work like that. You can't suddenly say you're going to be something, and then be it.' This was useless. The statues were never going to help.

'Why not?' said the man. 'We do.'

'But you're magic. That's different.'

'Magic,' he whispered, 'is inside every single person . . .'

'. . . You simply have to use it,' finished the woman.

And without another word, both statues froze, hands on hips, looking straight ahead.

16

Ember and Hans stared at each other.

'What a waste of time!' Ember said. That hadn't helped at all and whatever the statues had thought, she didn't know how to use magic. Ember stared down at the clock. 00:45.

'Ember, the birds are here again,' said Hans, pointing back the way they had come.

Ember turned to see seven origami birds sitting in a line in the middle of the path. Their heads were all leaning to the left, seven sets of horrible reflective eyes staring at her. At home she had only ever seen one, but up here, they seemed to be multiplying.

'Maybe they're here to help, like they did in the Know-It-Hall?' said Ember, approaching the birds.

The origami bird in the middle flitted towards her, its beady eyes narrow and accusing. Then, as if it had heard her speak, it began to shake, unfolding until it lay flat. On the piece of white card was a message.

Tick tock. My, my, how time flies.

Ember had the strangest feeling, a sort of déjà vu.

But whatever it was, she didn't have time to think about it.

The card wasn't helping her, it was *warning* her.

She had to hurry. She turned back and rushed around the edge of the pool, charging her way towards the jars of talents.

There were so many of them; there had to be something here to help her. She crouched down next to where the waterfall crashed into the pool, droplets of the spray hitting her face. Carefully, she pulled out Juniper's clock. What talents would a clockmaker have?

Hans looked over her shoulder. 'Ember, do you think—'

'Hans, please be quiet. I need to find the right talents.'

'But the problem is . . .'

She looked up at Hans as he trailed off. He didn't look sad or sulky this time. He seemed unsure. That was worse, somehow.

'. . . I don't know if this is going to work,' he finished.

Ember swallowed down the lump building in her throat. 'It doesn't matter. I have to try. I *have* to.'

A half-smile appeared on Hans' face. He leant down and put his hand over Ember's. 'Then let's try together.'

She nodded and turned back to the jars, blinking back tears. There weren't many she could reach, lots of them were too high. But there had to be something.

Another origami bird fell in front of her, twisting down through the air, unfolding by the time it had reached the floor.

Tick tock. Tick tock.

She had to hurry.

17

Patience Potion. Confidence Confusion. Melodrama Mix.

Ember kept scanning the names on each bottle, but none of them seemed quite right. She kept looking, her heart thumping. There! *Ingenuity Infusion*. And there was another, *Creativity Coffee*. Ember pulled both of them down, balancing on her tiptoes to reach the second. The infusion was a bright purple colour, filling a long, thin tube all the way to the top. The coffee was golden, glimmering and shining in its glass mug like a jar full of fireflies.

She and Hans examined the jars. 'What do you think I do?' she asked.

'Drink them?' he said.

She brought the infusion to her nose, sniffing at it uncertainly.

'Let me!' he shouted. 'You don't know what these funny little bottles might do. It would be an honour to drink them for the great Ember Shadows.'

Ember smiled down at him, a wave of warmth crashing through her. She never would have guessed that a clock hand could make such a good friend – the greatest friend she'd ever had in fact. Apart from Juniper, of course.

'Thank you, Hans. But no. You're not human, they might not even work on you,' she said, squeezing his little fingers.

She tried to ignore the niggling voice inside telling her not to drink strange liquids. This was for Juniper.

She screwed her eyes closed and brought the tube of *Ingenuity Infusion* to her lips. As soon as it hit her tongue, it exploded. Fireworks erupted in her mouth, a strawberry flavour bursting with each *pop* and *bang*. As she swallowed, the liquid hissed all over her tongue and fizzed at her teeth, before zooming down her throat like a rocket.

She waited a few seconds.

'Do you feel any different?' whispered Hans.

Ember shook her head. She would have to try the *Creativity Coffee*, too.

This time at least she was ready for anything. A small sip of the golden liquid warmed her tongue. It spread all around her mouth and over her teeth, coating them like treacle. She ran her tongue around the inside of her cheeks, trying to prise it off the sides of her mouth, but within seconds it was gone.

Ember set her sister's clock on the ground. This was it. Inspiration would strike now. She would know exactly what to do.

She just had to wait.

She stared at the clock, trying to ignore Hans, who was jiggling nervously beside her. Every tick was one tock closer to Juniper's death. *Come on, Ember. Think!*

But she wasn't having any fantastic ingenious ideas. In fact, she didn't feel any different at all.

Hans opened his mouth, then closed it.

'What is it?' she said.

'I had an idea, but it's probably a bit silly,' he said. 'You're the one with the clever ideas, not me.'

Ember considered this. His 'ideas' *had* nearly turned them into bookworms not long ago. But she was running out of options. 'If it's an idea, then it's already more than I've got,' she said. 'Tell me.'

Hans beamed back at her. 'Maybe there's a talent you could put on the clock itself? Maybe then it would be fixed without our help?'

'That's a great idea, Hans!'

She could have sworn his metallic skin blushed in the sunlight. Together, they searched the wall until Ember spotted a larger jar. *Patcher Pitcher*.

'Patching things up, that's like fixing them, right?' she asked. Hans shrugged.

'I guess,' he said.

She grabbed the jar from the wall. It was about the size of a water jug, and inside was a silvery metallic liquid, a similar colour to her toolkit. The liquid was bubbling as though it was hot, but the glass was cold to touch. Kneeling down, Ember set the jar on the grass and unscrewed the back casing from the pocket watch, revealing the broken wheel.

She turned it as best she could, along with the wheel that was still intact, lining up the hands of the clock. She lined them up to seven and eight. Seventy-eight was a good age; Juniper herself had said that. It was much better than eight anyway.

Ember paused for a second. *What if this made*

everything worse?

As though he could read her mind, Hans lifted up the clock. 'It's like you said, Ember Shadows. We have to try.'

With a deep breath, Ember unscrewed the jar and started to pour the bubbling liquid on to the clock. Then, carefully, Hans turned the clock over so the liquid could flow across the crack in the glass at the front as well. Once the liquid had covered the clock entirely, Ember stopped, took the clock from Hans and screwed the back casing on, trying not to touch the sticky silver substance as she placed the clock on the ground. And then they waited.

Gradually, the bubbling stopped. But nothing super magical seemed to be happening. Ember had been hoping for something obvious to happen, something big, something that said, 'Ember, you've done it!'

Instead, the liquid started to move. It collected right in the centre of the clock face and formed a ball. The ball rolled towards the edge, then back into the centre, then to the edge again. The crack on the front faded completely, sewn together by the silver bubbles, and Ember's heart leapt. But then the silver ball of liquid rolled right off the clock, dropping on to the grass beneath her. Ember frowned.

The ball kept rolling, further and further away, until it stopped on the edge of the pool. It hovered for a split second and then plopped right into the water below.

Hans peered over to look at the clock. 'Did it work?'

The crack had disappeared completely, so that was good. And the hands were still where she had put them, on seven and eight.

Maybe. Maybe it *had* worked.

But as Ember picked the clock up, her heart in her throat, the hands fell from their position. The two slivers of metal went limp and hung at the bottom of the clock, swinging gently back and forth. Ember turned the clock over frantically. Where the tiny numbers had been counting down, it was now blank.

Had they stopped the countdown without fixing the clock? Without the numbers, it was impossible to know! And now Juniper had no age of death at all. What did *that* mean?

Ember screamed in frustration. Why was it all so difficult? She should never have bothered coming up the mountain, she should never have thought she could help Juniper, she should have realised that she was never destined for anything but an empty shell of a life.

She brought her knees up to her chest and buried her face in them. This was all such a stupid idea. She'd made everything worse, and now, now she might have done something terrible to Juniper.

Ember felt a tiny hand on her shoulder and looked up to see Hans smiling sadly at her.

'It's still ticking,' he said. 'That means we've still got time.'

Ember wiped her face and tried to grasp on to that tiny piece of hope, that it might not be too late.

Suddenly, Hans cried, 'Ember, a bird!'

From between the long branches of a willow tree, a large shape flew towards them. Instinctively, Ember grabbed Hans and pulled him close. The bird's wings spread wide as it cast a shadow over them, circled and came to land in front of Ember's feet, right next to Juniper's clock.

'Oh, please,' it said, ruffling its feathers as it took a step closer. Ember could see now that it wasn't a large origami bird but a real-life owl, a beautiful brown owl, the colour of milk chocolate, with flecks of black mixed in among its feathers. A pair of large hexagonal glasses rested on her beak. 'I'm not going to hurt you.'

Even so, Ember shuffled back on the grass. She had heard wild birds could be quite dangerous, although maybe this one wasn't wild. It was wearing glasses, after all.

'My name is Florence.' The owl stretched out a wing towards Ember. 'Pleasure to meet you. Was that Patcher Pitcher you poured on there?' she said, tilting her head towards the clock.

Ember nodded.

'Not the worst idea, I'll admit,' the owl squawked. 'And drinking the talents was a good idea, too. But you must have those gifts somewhere in you already, otherwise you would have felt a change.'

That didn't seem likely to Ember. If she had ingenuity and creativity within her, she'd have been able to fix this mess. 'Well it didn't work. So what do I do now? I'll never fix Juniper's clock if even magic as powerful as this doesn't work.'

Florence's bright green eyes narrowed. 'So you really *are* the girl.'

'What girl?'

'The girl the whole mountain has been talking about. The girl trying to save her sister and find a fate for herself! I must say, this will be brilliant in the first issue of *Mount Never News*! I'm starting a newspaper, you see. This can be front page.' From under her wing, Florence pulled a pocket notebook and pencil, and then pushed her glasses further up her beak. 'Mind if I ask you a few questions?'

'Yes, I do actually. I don't have time for this,' said Ember. She gathered up Juniper's clock and got to her feet. 'I have to get going.'

'Look, Ember. Another bird.' Hans whispered, pointing to the right side of the waterfall, where an origami bird stared down at them from the top of a jar.

'You haven't been trusting *those* birds, have you?' Florence leant forward.

'What do you mean?'

'Oh, my dear. *Look* at them! Paper bodies but living eyes, that's some dark magic at work there. There's so much you don't know.' She tucked her notebook back under her wing and moved closer. 'First of all, you won't be able to fix anything from down here – not your sister's fate nor your own.'

'Why not?'

'Because . . .' She leant closer, one eye on the origami bird as it took off and darted straight into the waterfall. '. . . those birds, they're from the top. And that means the Fateweaver knows exactly what you're up to.'

'Who?'

'The Fateweaver,' Florence said, as though Ember ought to know. Florence's eyes hardened, and she shook her feathered head. 'Oh, my dear, you're in a lot more trouble than you thought.'

18

Ember's mind boggled. The Fateweaver? She'd never heard of such a person.

'You must have heard on your way up that things used to be rather different around here,' said Florence. 'Everyone thinks you're here to fix the mountain.'

'But I'm not, I'm here to—'

'Yes, yes, I know what you have to do, and I know you're in a hurry, rushing here, there and everywhere,' Florence said as she sat down, her tiny bird feet sticking out in front of her. Ember had never seen a bird sit like that before. Then again, she'd never seen a bird talk before. 'But at least let me tell you what you're up against.'

Ember sighed. She had been charging headfirst into every realm but hadn't yet fixed anything. Maybe she *should* listen to Florence. She sat down opposite the bird and nodded at her to go on.

'For thousands of years, this mountain was free,' Florence began. 'Threads of Fate are created in the centre of the mountain, you see, and it used to be that when a human in your world was born, their thread would come out from the top. The threads used to fly up and down this mountain, zooming in and out of realms, picking up talents from this waterfall, changing their clocks in the Forest of Time, absorbing intelligence from the Know-It-Hall.'

'So what changed?'

'Well, someone stopped the threads, right at the top. They never come down any more. A person's fate used to change with every decision a person made, that's why the threads would zoom around the mountain. But now, the threads don't come down at all. People still have fates, but those fates don't change.'

'Who's stopping them?' asked Hans, mouth agape.

'Here on the mountain, we call them the Fateweaver,' said Florence darkly.

'But who *is* the Fateweaver? Where did they come from?' asked Ember.

Florence's eyes darted between them. 'No one knows . . . but that's not really the question you need to be asking, is it? Surely the question is *why*?'

It was a good point. Why would anyone want to fix people's fates? Why would that person make it Juniper's fate to die so young? And why make Ember's fate empty?

'Of course, I don't expect young ones like yourselves to think of questions like that,' said Florence, her head tilted back slightly. 'I am the wisest creature on this mountain, after all.'

'I wish I was wise,' said Hans with a sigh.

But Ember was still trying to piece it all together. 'So someone is fixing fates – but we don't know who. Do we know *how*?'

'Not exactly,' said Florence. 'Only that they seem to be taking the uncertainty out of life, so that all of you humans know exactly what will happen in your future. Rather takes the fun out of things if you ask me.'

'And the Fate Cards? The Fateweaver sends them?'

'Yes. Rather ingenious really.'

Ember tried to sort it all out in her head. It was so confusing. A mountain that made Threads of Fate. Some strange person on the top of the mountain, fixing the fates in place.

'Florence, if this Fateweaver person is fixing fates, does that mean people could have had other fates?'

'Well, of course. Everyone would have had thousands of different fates. But once the Fateweaver chooses a fate, all of the others become impossible to fulfil.'

'But why don't we get our cards when we're born then? Why do they take so long to come, if everything is decided?'

Florence let out a squawky chuckle. 'I'm not sure I'm the person to answer that question, my dear. But I suppose it's harder to cement a child's fate when they are very young because they're so full of dreams and imagination. As we get older, it's easy to forget all of that, and to let someone else plan your life for you.' She paused, and then looked carefully at Ember before continuing. 'Of course, there are people like yourself who never stop dreaming. I'd imagine your fate probably put up a bit more of a fight.'

'Is that why my Messy Middle was so messy? My fate is fighting back?'

'I think there's something different about you,' said Florence, laying her wing on Ember's knee. 'Your middle must have given that awful Moira woman quite the surprise.'

'She wasn't that awful to us.'

Florence ruffled her feathers. 'Terrible woman, she is. I can tell you, in my two hundred and thirty-seven years, I've never met someone quite like her. Came on to this mountain longer ago than I could tell you, pitched herself up in that realm and gave herself a job as conductor. There was no need for a conductor in the Messy Middle. Silly woman was just trying to escape the mess of a village she lived in.'

Ember was distracted by a movement from the corner of her eye. An origami bird that had been perching by the waterfall was flying off up into the sky, looking like it was in a hurry. Florence spotted it too and shook her head. 'There it goes, the little spy.'

'Spy? Flint said they were omens,' said Ember.

'Flint? Oh that oaf never was brave enough to leave his own patch of grass, not after he got stuck in the Know-It-Hall. He was too scared even to wait for his own card is what I heard,' said Florence. 'But not you. You're brave, aren't you, Ember?'

Ember shook her head. She didn't feel brave. 'Florence,' she said. 'How come *you've* never gone to see the Fateweaver? To find out who they are?'

The owl stood and hopped from one clawed foot to the other. 'I . . . well, I did try. Once.'

'What happened?'

'I got stuck, stuck in the next realm.' She shuddered. 'And I vowed I would never go back.'

Ember didn't like the sound of that. She swallowed and asked the question she didn't want the answer to. 'What is the next realm?'

'The Land of Fear.'

Now it was Ember's turn to shudder. A land dedicated to fear? Hope seemed to be diminishing with every second that Juniper's clock ticked on. She looked at Hans, whose face was etched with worry.

'We've got to try, Ember Shadows, haven't we?' he asked quietly. 'For Juniper?'

Ember stood up slowly and squared her shoulders. 'Yes,' she said. 'For Juniper.'

Hans' face spread into a huge grin. He shot up into the air, looping in circles above their heads. 'The adventure continues!' he yelled. 'Wooooooooo-eeeeeeeeee!'

19

Ember watched the waterfall crash into the pool below as she stood with Hans and Florence. There was a knot in her stomach that she was trying to ignore.

'Is this it?' she asked quietly. 'The gateway to the next realm?'

Florence nodded. 'In a way. This is the first of two gateways. The one into the Land of Fear itself can only be passed through alone. You'll see. It's up to each of us to make it through.'

'Us?'

'If I'm going to use this on the front page, I need to be there for the whole thing! Anyway, you clearly need my help.'

'Thank you,' said Ember. It seemed that no matter how many times she said she *didn't* need help or that it was *her* responsibility to save Juniper, neither Hans nor Florence was going to let her do this alone. So instead, Ember focused on the powerful, roaring waterfall ahead. 'You're absolutely sure the only way to get there is through *that*?' she asked.

Florence nodded and jumped up on to Ember's shoulder. Holding on to Hans' tiny hand, Ember and her new friends stepped into the pool and paddled towards the waterfall until they were so close that Ember could feel droplets on her skin.

'OK then, team,' said Hans. 'Let's do this!'

And with that, he pulled his hand from Ember's grip and leapt into the crashing cascade of colours that tumbled down the side of the wall.

Ember gulped. She wasn't as brave as Hans, especially when it came to water.

Florence's feathers brushed at Ember's cheek. 'Come on, we can do this bit at the same time,' she squawked. 'One, two, three . . .!'

With a deep breath, Ember squeezed her eyes closed as Florence took off from her shoulder, and she followed the owl into the downpour.

The liquid hit her like an ice curtain, and she couldn't help but gasp for air as her lungs tightened.

But it was over within a second.

When she opened her eyes again, she wasn't even damp. The water hadn't left a trace on her, nor on Florence's feathers or Hans' metallic skin.

'That wasn't so bad,' said Ember. She turned around. Instead of a waterfall, a tall red brick wall stood in its place, blocking their way back. The garden was nowhere to be seen. They were now in a very small room, bricked up on all four sides and even above them. The only things that weren't brick were the three doors straight ahead.

Hans was already bopping between the doors, looking at each in turn. One was an unpainted wooden oak door; the second was made of stripy bright blue and yellow metal; and the last was a smooth burnt-orange glass. Each had a brass door knocker carved into the shape of a face. The one on the wooden door had ears nearly as big as his face, the one on the stripy door had a chin that looked ready to drop off and the knocker on the orange door had a great big nose that drooped down like the curve of a banana.

'They look angry,' said Ember as she walked to the blue and yellow door. 'And ugly.'

Suddenly, all three door knockers came to life, their solid faces softening into live expressions. *Oh no.*

'Well, how very rude!' said the face with the chin.

Ember felt herself turning bright red.

'Quite,' said the one with the ears.

'Sorry, I didn't mean—'

But they were chattering between themselves, their clunky metallic voices growing louder and faster until Ember couldn't tell who was saying what. She could hear snippets of 'rude' and 'ugly' and 'well if I had a face as red as hers I wouldn't be saying anything'.

A loud cough filled the room. Thank goodness for Florence.

'If you don't mind, gentlemen, we're on a bit of a schedule. Could you let us through?'

The left and right door faces turned to look at the head on the orange door.

'Indeed, indeed,' the knocker said, clearing his throat. 'Welcome to the Land of Fear.'

The other heads turned back to face them, each one stern and angry, and Ember felt the hairs on her neck begin to tingle. Each head seemed to have chosen one of them to stare at. The one speaking was looking at Ember, the knocker with elephant-sized ears was glaring at Florence, and the last had chosen Hans. 'Behind these doors are your greatest fears, fears beyond even your worst nightmares.'

Hans looked up at Ember, eyes wide, then back at the doors.

'Each of you must face your fears alone. Only when you confront the fear and find the key will you be released.'

'The key?' said Ember. 'What key?'

'A key has been hidden deep inside your fear. To leave the realm, simply touch the key. Until you do . . . you will remain in the Land of Fear.'

'Can't we go together?' asked Hans in a small voice. He edged closer until Ember could feel his tiny hand against her leg.

'No,' said the one with the big chin. Ember didn't like the way he was staring at Hans, like he was going to eat him. 'You're mine, you have to go through my door. And you have to do it alone.'

Ember looked down at the others. What had she got them into? She bit her lip and tucked her hair behind her ears as she crouched down. Hans and Florence stared back at her, their faces etched with worry.

'Florence, can you tell us about when you came before?' whispered Hans. 'It might make us feel braver.'

'I don't think that's a good idea,' said Florence. Her eyes were on the floor. 'I was in there a long time. But we're a team now. Back then I was on my own. Even though we'll be in different places, we'll all be going through it together. Let's try to remember that.'

'Look,' said Ember. 'You two don't have to come. It's my sister we're trying to save, not yours. I can go through and you two can go back.'

Hans put his hand on Ember's knee. 'It will be a super-duper honour to face my fears for Ember Shadows.'

'And I'll have the best front-page story I could hope for,' said Florence.

Ember opened her mouth to speak, but before she could say anything, Hans spun around, began bouncing up and down and screamed at the top of his voice. 'Charge!'

He ran straight towards the blue-and-yellow striped door, which flung itself open and then slammed shut behind him.

Florence and Ember stared after him for a moment in stunned silence.

'I suppose it's time to get going,' said Florence.

They lined up at their doors. Florence waved a feathered goodbye and headed through her brown wooden door. Ember stepped forward.

But as she crossed the boundary between realms, she could have sworn she heard the distant sound of a spluttering engine, crashing water, and a familiar voice shouting her name.

20

It wasn't the darkness that scared her.

It wasn't even not knowing what was hiding *under* the darkness.

No, it was the familiar smell that lingered in the air. It was the same scent that filled Ember's home after a storm, the smell of the thatched roof after it had been rained on. Usually, it was a smell that comforted her. But here, the smell crept into her nose and suffocated her.

It didn't belong *here*.

Her eyes strained to find a shape in the dark. Was there someone there? A person behind the voice she had heard? She didn't dare move; she couldn't see her feet, let alone what was beneath them.

Then, slowly, the darkness started to clear, like a cloud passing through the sky, revealing a building in front of her. Rounded walls, tall thatched roof, dark red door – this was the reason for that familiar smell. Her home.

Seeing it here didn't give her any comfort. She swallowed, her mouth dry. Lightning struck the sky above her, but there was no sound of thunder. It was completely silent. Even when she stepped on to the gravel path, her feet didn't make a noise.

Her hand hesitated as it reached the door. Then, as the lightning flashed again around her, she pushed.

Laughter came from somewhere inside, breaking the silence. Somehow, it was worse than the sobs she had heard coming from Juniper's room the day she got her card.

She had to go slowly. She couldn't rush and forget where she was. This was the Land of Fear after all, she couldn't run at the first sound of laughter and fall into a trap.

Carefully, she closed the door behind her, and that's when she saw it.

The family frame that held the Fate Cards was on the wall, just like it was in their house. But it was different. Juniper's card was in the frame as well as her father's. And there was no empty space for hers.

Somewhere deep down, Ember had known exactly what her greatest fear was, but seeing the frame filled like that, without her card alongside her sister's, it was as though the world had tilted and she was falling right off it, disappearing into oblivion. A single word filled all the cards, over and over and over again, taunting her: *happy, happy, happy, happy.* And in the centre of Juniper's, her number had changed to a hundred.

Tears stung Ember's eyes. This was what their life would have been without her. If Dad had never saved her that day, if she had died instead of him. And now it was all being played out right before her.

Juniper's laugh filled the hallway, rattling Ember's thoughts.

She had to keep going. Her sister's card might say one hundred in this warped land, but it wasn't real. The real Juniper was dying, and it was up to Ember to save her.

Ember followed the corridor around the house to the kitchen. *The key.* She had to look for the key. She pushed open the door, bracing herself for whatever was on the other side. But there was no one in there.

The small table at the back had place settings made out for three people, but she knew none of them were for her. A picture on the wall hung over the table. It was almost like the picture she had in her bag, the one with her and Juniper on their parents' shoulders. In *this* version, Ember had disappeared and, instead, Juniper was on Mum's shoulders, Dad squeezing them into a hug. All their arms were wrapped around each other, limbs tangled together.

She looked away but she could feel them staring at her as she searched for the key, opening and closing cupboard doors, peering under the sink. Her eye caught on the frame. She had to check everywhere. She pulled it from the wall, but there was no key behind it.

The laughter continued. It grew louder as she crept back into the hallway and towards the living room. The door was already open; she could see the light spilling out from the room. Ember turned to face it and a terrible ache began in her chest.

They were all there. Mum and Dad on the sofa, Juniper sitting on the floor in front of them. Dad was exactly how she remembered him, his messy hair the same shade as hers, creeping over the tops of his ears, his wrinkled face permanently in a smile, his arms around Mum. Ember couldn't remember seeing Mum so happy, not in a long time. She was working her fingers through Juniper's hair, plaiting it into two neat braids.

None of them said a word as Ember stepped forward, trance-like.

She missed him so much. Every single day since the accident. She missed the way he smiled at her and Juniper, the way he burnt eggs every time he tried to make breakfast, the way he would scoop her up on to his shoulders and show her how the world might look if she were a giant.

Something snapped in her and Ember ran forward, past Juniper, past Mum and straight to him. She reached her arms out – finally she could hug him again, finally she could –

'Dad!'

No.

She fell straight through him on to the sofa. He disappeared like a gust of steam and was gone.

'Dad? No, Dad, where are you?' she stammered. Her face was hot and she could feel the tears on her cheeks.

Juniper turned to her, bright blue eyes wide. 'Ember, what have you done?'

'I didn't do anything.' She stood up, stumbling as she did. 'Juniper, I, I just wanted to hug him, I—'

'Ember, this is all your fault.'

'No, Juniper, I'm sorry, please, I—' Her voice cracked as she staggered back.

'Ember Shadows?'

Hans' voice floated through the air.

'Ember? Are you there?'

Juniper didn't seem to have heard anything – her eyes were still locked on to Ember. But Hans' voice had reminded Ember that this wasn't real. It was a nightmare. And if Hans was calling her name, then maybe he needed her. Her friends needed her. Juniper needed her.

She had to find the key.

Ember sprinted out of the room and back to the hallway. She stopped at the bedrooms. There were only two – that made sense, there was no need for a third without Ember. The door to the first was open, and Ember ran inside, searching through her mum's and dad's things, tipping them up and emptying boxes. Nothing.

The second bedroom door had a window, and as she reached it, dread filled her body like a sickness.

On the other side of the glass, inside Juniper's bedroom, water filled the room to the ceiling. Juniper's blanket swam past the door, while at the bottom of the room, her shoes, boxes and trinkets had sunk to the ground like lost treasure.

There, right in the centre of all that treasure, was a golden key, glinting from the mess.

Ember sank down, her back against the door, and hugged her knees to her chest.

Even with her back turned, she could feel the water beating against the door, the rise and fall of the waves thundering through her. She had that seasick feeling, of being pulled down into the current.

There was no way she could do this. It was impossible. The second she opened that door, the water would pour over her like a tidal wave and then what? She hadn't swum since the day at the river. *That* day.

Before then, she had been one of the strongest swimmers at school. Her class would go down to the river each week and practise, as long as the current wasn't too strong. It was about fifty metres from one bank to the other, and Ember was almost always the fastest to reach the other side. She would even make her parents take her down at the weekend. She was only six, but she loved it. The feeling of the water pulling you gently one way and then the other.

The thought made her feel sick now.

Ember stood back up and faced the door.

She would die in all that water. It would pull her straight under like the current had done that day, and this time Dad wouldn't be there to save her. Ember reached down to her ankle where her foot had been caught in the rocks. She still had the scar.

But if she didn't go in, if she didn't reach that key, who would save Juniper?

There was nothing she could do about Dad now. But she could do something about her sister.

Ember tightened the straps on her backpack. She reached out and grabbed hold of the door handle. As she pushed it down, the door was ripped from her grip and flung wide open.

The tide flooded over her in an instant and Ember was knocked off her feet. The water was everywhere, all around her, in her eyes, flinging her from one side of the hallway to the other. Her chest tightened in panic as she was spun by the water; there was no way of telling which way was up or down.

Somehow she found herself at the surface for a second and gasped a breath in, but before she could take another one, something gripped her. It pulled her down and water filled her ears, muffling the crashing of the waves.

She was going to die.

Ember thrashed around, her arms desperately trying to grip on to something, her legs flailing underneath her as the water rushed through the hallway, circling the house like a deadly rapid. The water kept pouring out of Juniper's room, faster and faster, rising higher and higher.

She reached out, trying to grab on to the open door to Juniper's room. She must have been swept past it twice already. Her fingers slipped and she fell back into the water, her body too weak to hold on. The water pulled her round again, past the kitchen and the living room where Juniper and her mum sat like a freeze-frame. If she could just get to the surface. She spluttered, gasping for air.

Again she reached out for the door. This time she got hold of the frame. Ember pulled her legs forward to cling on to the edge of it like a monkey and climbed towards the top as the rapids crashed into her, each wave trying to prise her from safety.

Ember emerged from the water, gasping. She could hear the water in her ears, the pounding of her blood smashing through her head. She was shaking and the cold was biting into her skin. Her thighs ached as she gripped the doorframe with her knees and arms, every muscle tense, clinging on as best she could.

The key.

She had to get the key, then it would all stop.

The rapids that were circling the hallway were still rising, higher and higher, threatening to pull her back down into the watery storm. And they were just one of the dangers. Ember stared into the whirlpool that had once been Juniper's bedroom, horrified. The water seemed to be infinite. The deep flood in the hall was still rising, but it had done nothing to lower the water in the bedroom. Inside the room, the water had whipped itself into a watery tornado that started at the ceiling and narrowed right down to the floor, where a single golden key lay on the ground.

If Ember wanted the key, she was going to have to let go and dive headfirst, right into the whirlpool.

The water in the hallway kept surging. It was already at her shoulders as she clung halfway up the doorframe. She had no choice, she had to jump, or she would drown.

She knew what she had to do.

With a deep breath, Ember clenched her eyes closed and leapt into the whirlpool.

Her body was pulled one way, then the other, and she couldn't see a thing. There was nothing to grab to steady herself. Her arm was snapped back, then her leg, and she was turned upside-down, then spun around right side up. Eyes wide, she searched for the key.

There. A glimmer of gold. She could see it as she hurtled round in the spiral.

She started moving her arms and legs, kicking with her ankles, pulling the water back as hard as she could with her arms, forcing herself to swim. No matter what happened, she had to keep swimming towards the key.

Her lungs burned but she was getting closer. She was doing it. One more stroke. She could almost reach it . . .

With a final kick, Ember stretched out her right hand and felt the air as her fingers broke through to the centre of the whirlpool. The feeling of cold metal met her skin.

Then, everything went black.

21

'Ember? Ember, can you hear me?' a soft, gentle voice was asking.

'EMBER SHADOWS!' yelled a much louder voice. 'WAKE UP!'

Ember blinked her eyes open to see Hans' face inches from hers, and Florence staring down at them from above.

'YES!' screamed Hans. 'Whooooopppeeeee! She's alive! The great EMBER SHADOWS is alive!' Florence flew down and landed beside them.

Ember sat up and brushed off her knees. Somehow, she was completely dry – even her bag was dry, as though she'd never been in the water at all.

'You both made it,' she said. 'Are you OK?'

They nodded back at her. She must have taken a lot longer to get past her fears than they had.

'The question is, where are we?' said Hans.

Ember looked around. They were in some sort of

forested area, no trace of the Land of Fear at all. A path wound from the small clearing where they sat off through the shrubs and trees ahead. The moon hung close over them. So, it was night again. Time didn't seem to stick to the rules up here.

'I think we're nearly there,' said Florence.

The forest was wild around them. Roots and vines criss-crossed the floor, leaves scattered across them. Each tree stretched up towards the moon, fighting its way past the surrounding plants. Ember felt the weight of a pair of eyes on her back and had the ominous feeling that she was being watched again. She couldn't see any little white birds, but the feeling was there.

'Did you hear someone shout my name?' she asked. 'Before we went in, I thought I heard someone.'

They shook their heads.

'Strange. How long have you both been out?'

'I got out first,' smiled Hans. His chest swelled with pride. 'It was pretty scary though, Ember.' His eyes were wide, tiny eyelashes unblinking as he spoke. 'I had to go through a world where the clocks were all missing their hands! *None* of them had hands. None at all! It was *horrible*.' He shuddered.

'Well, mine was even more frightful,' said Florence, as she shifted from one clawed foot to the other. 'I had no feathers and I was freezing, freezing to death in a world filled with ice.'

'That sounds awful,' whispered Ember.

'It was, and do you want to know the worst bit? The truly worst part? There was nobody there! It was so lonely, and terribly dull. Can you imagine? Nobody to tell me their secrets, nobody to talk to, nobody to chatter with. A world without any gossip at all. No wonder I had time to freeze half to death. Anyway, what was yours?'

She would have to tell them; she couldn't lie after they had revealed their own fears to her.

So she told them everything: the way her sister had looked when her dad had disappeared, the way the water had ripped around the house, the way she'd finally broken through the whirlpool. When she finished, no one said a word.

'I feel a bit, you know . . . a bit bad,' she said quietly. 'My greatest fear should be Juniper dying, shouldn't it? But it was my family being happier without me.'

'You can't help what your fear is,' said Hans.

'No,' added Florence. 'You're fearing Juniper's death right now too because she's in danger. But your deepest, darkest fear, that's the one that keeps you up at night, the one that defines who you are. Only when you face that fear can you possibly hope to stand up to everything else.'

Hans reached his arm up and patted hers. 'Like my super scary clocks,' he said. 'You're lucky you don't have to face *those*.'

Florence and Ember burst into laughter; they couldn't help it. Hans looked from one of them to the other, bewildered.

'Come on,' said Ember. 'We have to hurry. There's no way of knowing how long Juniper's got left now. We can't sit around here.'

With Florence flitting from tree to tree, and Hans bobbing alongside her, she started on the path.

'Ember, dear,' said Florence from above, 'if you don't mind me asking – why are you scared of water? I know it's terribly nosy of me to ask. We can keep it off the record if you like.'

Ember bit her lip. She understood why they would want to know, but still, it was hard to talk about it.

'I nearly drowned once, when I was little,' she said. 'We were all down by Border River and I was practising my swimming, but the current was stronger than we realised. I got pulled under and my ankle got stuck between two rocks.' She looked down at her feet as they pounded the path. This was the hard part. 'Dad jumped in and had to dive to get my ankle out of the rocks. But when he was pushing me up to the bank, he got dragged under himself. They got him out and tried to save him . . . but nothing worked.'

'I bet your dad was an amazing, super, wonderful, marvellous man,' said Hans. 'Just like you.'

Florence looked down at them and then flew off to the next branch. 'That's a very tragic story, dear. I am sorry for your loss. And don't worry, we can keep it out of the paper.' She pretended to zip up her beak with her feathers.

'Thank you. That's why I've got to save Juniper. I've got to save her and find a fate for myself, otherwise Dad died for nothing and—'

'Sorry, Ember,' said Hans, interrupting her as they turned a bend in the path. 'But what's that?'

Ahead of them was a well. It had a wooden frame

above it, from which a rope dangled down into the hole below.

Ember peered over the edge and instead of finding a bucket at the end of the rope, she saw her own face reflected back at her, so clear and so pure she could have been looking into a mirror.

'*Well-Wouldn't-You-Like-To-See*,' read Hans, from a copper plaque attached to the front of the well that Ember hadn't noticed. 'What do you think that means?'

Suddenly, the water trembled, and words began to form on the surface, inky and black.

It means this well shows you what you would like to see, whenever you would like to see it, past, present or future.

'Juniper,' said Ember, without a single hesitation. 'Is Juniper OK?'

With another tremble, the words disappeared and Juniper's face came into focus instead. For a second, relief flooded Ember. But something was wrong. Juniper was in bed. Her face was so pale, it was almost grey. Her eyes were surrounded by dark circles.

'Is that . . .' whispered Hans.

'That's Juniper,' Ember said. Her heart was pounding.

Juniper coughed and Ember noticed she was sweating. She looked sick, really sick. Who knew how long she had left?

'How long have we been up here, Hans?'

'Time is very different on the mountain,' he said. 'It's only been a few hours up here, but it will have been days down there.'

Ember's stomach dropped. She had missed what might be her last birthday with her sister. 'We have to find this Fateweaver and fix everything, and we have to do it *now*.'

'Well, I think you might get the chance soon enough,' said Florence from a treetop. 'I can see the wooden building, where the Fateweaver lives, up ahead. We're almost there.'

Ahead, the mountain came to a point, and the miraculous wooden building sat on top like a seesaw, framed by the moon behind. Ember had spent so many hours staring up at it from her treehouse, and now here it was, its long base stretched out over the tiny peak, balanced like a set of scales. It looked as though a single raindrop falling on one end would tip it over and send it plunging down through the carpet of clouds that surrounded them.

'That's a big door,' whispered Hans.

From the top of the building's flat roof, a chimney stuck out into the sky at an angle, as though it had been added as an afterthought. Two glass windows stared at them like eyes, each made of tiny bits of colourful glass in a mosaic of shattered pieces. And, right in the centre, directly above the peak of the mountain, was the giant door that Hans had pointed out.

Surely, Ember thought, when that door opened, the balance of the building would shift and that would send it hurtling off down the side of the mountain. She went through every calculation she could think of, but she couldn't see any way that it would work.

The three of them stood in silence, staring at the building.

Ember had finally made it to the top. This was her chance – her chance to save Juniper and fix her own fate, standing right before her on the very tip of the mountain.

But rather than charging forward, running headfirst at it, she was stuck, glued to the path.

'Come on, Ember! Let's go and save your sister,' called Hans, raising his fist as he jumped forward.

She grabbed hold of his arm, pulling him back. 'Hans, we have to be careful. We don't know what it's going to be like in there.'

'She's right,' said Florence. 'Even your weight could shift the building and we'd all be plummeting downwards faster than you could say Mount Never.'

'What's the other option?' Hans looked up at them.

But neither of them had a better plan.

Ember chewed the inside of her cheek as she weighed up what to do. 'OK. But, Hans, stay behind me. And Florence, it's probably best if you stay in the air. Let's try and think super light thoughts.'

Hans nodded energetically, and slowly, carefully, the three of them edged up the path towards the impossibly balanced house.

22

At the front of the building, two steps lay between them and the door. The mountain was so steep and so narrow that they had to huddle close together not to fall straight off it. Carefully, Ember put one foot on the first step, right in the middle. The house didn't budge. Closing her eyes, she raised her other foot off the ground and stood fully on the step.

The house was still.

One more step up, and Ember had her hand on the door.

'You can do it,' whispered Hans.

She spread both hands as wide as she could to balance the force and pushed. A groan came from the hinges as it opened, just a crack.

Still, the house didn't move.

As Ember pushed the door open further and further, her confidence began to grow. The house wasn't going to move. They were safe, for now. She stepped through the open door, Hans and Florence following behind.

The building seemed even larger on the inside. A single room stretched right across from one wall to the other, the entire ceiling hidden by what looked like a sort of web, made from thousands of threads. Every thread was unique – some were thick, some brightly coloured, some plaited through with others, all criss-crossed like a huge nervous system above their heads. Each one seemed to be trying to burrow through the walls, as if desperately trying to flee the building. But in the middle of the room, keeping them prisoner, holding every thread fixed in place, was an enormous machine.

It was a giant rectangular block, juddering quietly as it worked. On the left end of the machine, a funnel pointed out to the side. This was where all the hundreds of threads were emerging from. But the machine was holding on to them, stopping them from escaping the building, like a child clinging to thousands of kite strings. A chimney on the machine's top side fought through the net of threads to the roof, and on the side facing Ember were dozens of dials all over the red metal. Each one was still, even as the device trembled.

As she stepped forward, Ember spotted something out of the corner of her eye. A single thread was shooting around the ceiling above them. It was weaving itself into the web of threads, then pulling back out and going another way. It was like a loose hair in the wind, zapping around and then back under, right through the centre and then out again. Somehow, it had escaped the funnel. It was free.

'Where's the Fateweaver?' whispered Hans.

Ember shrugged, looking around. Apart from the machine, there was a desk in the corner, stacked tall with thousands of pieces of white card. Next to the desk, she could see an old brown bucket of glimmering liquid; Ember knew it had come from the Well-Wouldn't-You-Like-To-See. Its wood was the same kind as the frame above the well, where the bucket should have hung.

Above the desk, a circle had been fixed to the wall. There was a single clock hand pointing down to where the six would have been on a normal clock, but there were no numbers, only a single, unmoving hand pointing down at the messy desk.

There was nothing else in the room. And *no one* else either. A smile spread across Ember's face. The

Fateweaver wasn't here. This would be easier than she had thought.

'You two keep a lookout, OK?'

Ember didn't wait for them to protest. Instead, she crouched down and crept towards the machine, her ears pricked for any sign of the Fateweaver's return. Every step was a gamble. She tried not to think about how carefully the building was balanced on the mountain as she swung her backpack round to the front to pull out the silver case of tools her dad had given her. As quietly as possible, she took a screwdriver out and zipped up the backpack.

'Ember!' called Hans in a dangerously loud whisper. 'The clock! Have you seen it? It's amazing, that hand—'

'Shh!' she said. Now was *not* the time to be admiring clocks.

She made her way round to the back of the machine, ducking under the funnel as she went. There, she spotted a peculiar little window. Inside, at the back, was a pile of white Fate Cards; a single one had been pulled to the front. Across the top, a name had been typed. *Hortensia Thistlemore.* She was one of the girls from the village. Beneath the card, there was a single navy woollen thread, which stretched out from one side of the window to the other.

Below, two keyboards had been fitted to the machine. The first had the numbers 0-9, and a single button with the word *Balance*, which looked faded from overuse. The second keyboard appeared to be older, and had all the letters of the alphabet as well as some more buttons: *Input, Edit, Edit All.*

Ember narrowed her eyes. It was time to pull all the puzzle pieces together, and figure this out. From what Florence had told her, these threads must be the Threads of Fate, so this machine must be what was fixing them in place; that's why they couldn't escape through the walls and travel around Mount Never like they were supposed to. She bit her lip. That meant if she could break the machine, she would free the threads, surely?

But another idea began to niggle in her mind. Hortensia was the same age as Juniper, and as far as Ember knew, she hadn't got her card yet. That meant that her fate was still free, for now – clearly the machine was about to set her destiny.

So, maybe she could use Hortensia's card to see how the machine worked, first?

Her hand hovered above the *Balance* button. It was obviously the button pressed the most, so if she wanted to see what this machine did, it made sense to press it. Or should she simply jam her screwdriver in the machine and free everybody's fates?

Her fingers tightened around the tool in her hand as she fought with her curiosity.

Her hand reached out as she went to push the button.

A deafening, thunderous *POP* filled the air.

'Ember!' shouted Hans.

She jumped. Her hand slipped.

The machine juddered next to her and she looked down; she had pressed the number nine.

Hans and Florence rushed over to her, Florence landing by her feet, Hans clinging to her leg.

Then all three of them stared in shocked silence at Moira, who had appeared on the other side of the machine.

'Moira?' shouted Ember above the noise. '*You're* the Fateweaver? But you—'

'Were so nice and kind and such a fabulous tour guide?' Moira said, holding open what Ember now realised was a trapdoor in the floor. Ember shuddered.

If Moira thought she and her friends were going through that door willingly, she was very much mistaken. 'Well, I couldn't let you go through that realm alone. Judging by how you were getting on in the other realms, I'm surprised you made it up here to be honest. But you're here now, and that's all that matters.'

It all made sense now. Moira's anger at Ember's Messy Middle. That déjà vu when Ember had read the Fate Card. *My, my, how time flies.* Ember knew who spoke like that.

Moira's face, which had been odd-looking even in the dark of the Messy Middle, was even stranger now. The skin had been pulled too tight over her bones. Her smile was fixed into place. Everything about her was stiff, wooden. The only thing alive was the anger burning in her eyes.

'Anyway,' she said. 'You might want to worry more about *that*, than me.'

She nodded her head towards the machine, and Ember tore her eyes away from Moira to the tiny window, where a row of miniature mechanical arms was tapping away at Hortensia's card, filling it with words, while a single larger metal arm printed a great big number eighty-seven in the middle, before *whoosh!* The card was sucked up the chimney. The thread from the window shot out of the funnel, where one end immediately attached to a wall and began to try and escape; the other end was still trapped in the machine.

'My, my, you've pressed the wrong button, you silly little girl.' Moira's grin grew wider. 'And now, now we take another ride together.'

Ember glanced down at Hans and Florence, who were looking up at her expectantly. They were frightened. They trusted her to have a plan, but she had nothing.

Then the building started to move.

It was swaying, gently at first, but then with more power, forward and back, tipping like a seesaw on the top of the mountain.

What had she done?

The swaying grew stronger. Ember stumbled and Hans grabbed her leg as Florence began to flap, trying to balance as they rocked. Ember wasn't going to be able to stay upright much longer. The floor tipped again, forward this time, like a boat rolling over a huge wave.

She grabbed at the machine as the building tilted

down. 'Hold on!' she shouted to Hans and Florence. The building pitched backwards. She managed to grip on to part of the machine with her fingertips, but she wouldn't be able to hold on for long.

Her stomach lurched as the building swung again, back to the centre and then over. Moira hadn't even moved. She seemed glued in place. Cards that had been piled on the desk whizzed around her, sliding with the building each time it seesawed back and forth.

Hans let out a shriek. Florence clung on to the back of Ember's jacket and flapped, trying to pull her up. The building had tilted so far that Ember was swinging in thin air, the floor nearly vertical beneath her. She knew she couldn't hold on much longer, she was going to fall. And right below her was Moira's trapdoor!

Everything dipped further and the backs of her heels skidded on the floor as she held tight. If they slid through the trapdoor, they would tumble out into the clouds and down on to the mountain! She couldn't let that happen. Not when they were so close to fixing everything.

The building jerked back towards the centre. Suddenly her toes could touch the floor. Her knees buckled and she lost hold of the machine and fell down, almost on top of Florence. The building reached the horizontal point, but before Ember could get back on her feet, it had teetered past it. Ember grabbed Hans and Florence and pulled them close to her as they all skidded across the floor to the other end of the building, where Ember's head thudded against the wall. Moira stood, completely vertical, right above them, defying gravity as she held the trapdoor open next to her.

'You're mine!' she crowed.

Ember hugged Hans and Florence closer as the building began to tip back.

'Close your eyes,' she shouted, screwing her own shut as they plummeted feet first towards the Fateweaver and the open trapdoor.

23

'Hold on!' she screamed, ready for the long drop to certain death down the side of the mountain.

But no sooner had she finished shouting, than they hit solid ground.

'Is everyone OK?' said Ember, as she looked around, trying to take in their surroundings. The building had stopped tipping.

Hans carefully stretched out each metal limb. 'All fine,' he said.

But as Florence tried to flap, she cringed. 'My wing, oh my poor wing.' Ember reached forward to inspect it closer, but Florence shook her head. 'Don't worry, dear. I'm all right for now. We've got bigger things to worry about.'

'Where are we?' whispered Hans.

Ember didn't know. She had thought they would fly right out of the building and into thin air, so in some ways it was a relief to be on solid ground. But the space was small, a tiny wooden room with a flickering oil lamp in the corner.

She looked up. Far above them, Moira's face stared down from the trapdoor.

'Ember Shadows, welcome to the top of Mount Never.'

Anger boiled in Ember's stomach. 'Let us out of here, right now,' she said. She stood up, desperate to appear bigger and stronger to her enemy.

'Now, now, calm down. I'll explain everything – it's just, it's rather exciting!' Moira let out a joyful squeal. 'Finally, you're here.'

'You *wanted* me here?' said Ember.

Moira lay down, her hands resting on the edge of the trapdoor, her chin resting on her hands. She looked like a child, playing with her prisoners.

'Of course I wanted you here. Why do you think I made your sister's fate so terrible? Why do you think I helped you through that Messy Middle? And without my help in the Know-It-Hall, you probably wouldn't have made it in time.'

'*Your* help? What did you do to help me? I got here all by myself.'

'Don't be silly now, Ember,' said Moira, rolling her eyes. Then she let out a single, low whistle. One of the folded birds flapped into view and landed on Moira's shoulder.

'Surely you must have figured out that these birds are mine, yes? I've been watching you for quite some time now, ever since that terrible accident with your father. You see, nearly a century ago, I figured out that I could use the water from the Well-Wouldn't-You-Like-To-See to spy on Everspring. But I didn't like being stuck watching the well when there was so much to do. So I made my little birds, and I created their eyes from a drop of the well's water. I tell them what I want to see, and off they fly. When they come back, they show me what they've found. Until you came around, there hadn't been much to watch, but we've had quite good fun spying on you.'

She stroked the bird's long beak with her finger and gazed into its beady eyes.

Ember bristled. All this time, she had thought there was something wrong with her, that she was a freak. But really it had been Moira, watching, spying, and waiting.

'Without our help in the Know-It-Hall,' Moira continued, 'you'd never have made it through.'

'That's not true. Hans knew the answer!'

Moira shrugged and the bird hopped to her other shoulder. 'Maybe, but he was taking far too long.'

'But why do you want me here in the first place?'

Moira clicked her fingers and the origami bird flew headfirst into the wall, where it exploded into tiny slivers of paper.

'It's obvious, isn't it?' she said. A squeal burst from her lips and she clapped her hands together. 'Your fate can't be fixed, so I brought you here to give you a chance like no other. You're going to be my apprentice!'

Ember thought for a second she must have misheard. Surely this woman couldn't be serious? She couldn't truly think that Ember was going to help her, after what she had done to Juniper.

'Apprentice?'

'Exactly!' said Moira, grinning down at her excitedly. 'I couldn't let you live down in the village with no fixed fate – who knows what kind of mess you would have caused! No – I had to get you up here, to be sure that I could control what happened to your life. To begin with, I thought I'd trap you here, but after watching you for a while, I had a better idea. You could be my apprentice! You see, I realised something. You and me, we're the same.'

'But why would I work with you? After what you did to Juniper, and what you did to my father—'

'That was *your* fault, actually.'

'It wasn't,' Ember said. But she could hear the crack in her voice. 'It was his fate. *You* did that.'

'Me?' Moira laughed, the sound of it like broken shards of glass mixing together. 'No, under the fate *I* chose for him, the one my machine gave him, your father was destined to live a long life with the rest of your family. But when you were drowning, that meddling man wanted so desperately to save *you* that his Thread of Fate broke free from my machine, sending his fate in an entirely different direction.'

Ember's mouth was dry. She could feel the stillness in the air. Everything she had ever feared was true.

'That same day, your thread escaped the machine too, before I had even managed to assign it a fate. I desperately tried to catch it, but when I realised it wouldn't be caught, I started watching you instead. I've seen the way you invent things like I do, the way you've been hoping for a fate for years, the way you want people to be happy – we're so similar! And now that I've finally got you here, well, we're going to do great things together.'

The thought of working with Moira sent a chill down Ember's neck. As she watched, the smile faded from Moira's face, and Ember thought she could see a flicker of a real person, someone she used to be.

'It has been ever so lonely,' Moira whispered. 'Apart from the birds, it's just been me. You know, a hundred years is a long time to live alone. Now I've got you here, I don't have to be alone any more.'

The blood began to curdle around Ember's throat, anger rising like an eruption over any sympathy she had felt. 'You really think, after everything you've done, that I'm going to be your apprentice?'

Moira's face instantly switched back to the cold, hard stare. 'Of course you are, because that's the deal. You become my apprentice and promise to stay with me here, and I'll save your sister.'

'And if I refuse?'

'Your sister only has twenty-five minutes left,' Moira

said, spitting the words out. 'If you refuse, I'll let her die, then I'll chop her thread to bits for good measure. As for you, you'll be trapped here for the rest of your life. It's the only way I can be sure of what will happen to you.'

The threat hung in the air.

'You have ten minutes to decide.'

Moira slammed the trapdoor closed and her footsteps faded above.

Apart from the faint flickering glow of the oil light, they were in darkness.

Ember sank back against the wall. The weight of it all suddenly hit her like a train; she had tried so hard, but it hadn't counted for anything. In fact, she had only made things worse.

Now she was faced with a single solution: save her sister, but never see her again.

Tears stung her eyes as she looked at Hans, and then Florence. Not only had she failed, she had trapped her friends, too. Who knew what Moira would do with them? She only needed Ember, after all.

'I'm so sorry I dragged you both into this,' she said, the tears beginning to roll down her face. 'We're stuck here and it's all because of me.'

Hans shuffled over and put his hand on her knee.

'It's exactly as I've always thought,' Ember said. 'Dad's death *was* my fault. If it weren't for me, he would still be alive and Juniper wouldn't be dying.'

No one said a word. Ember could hear the blood pumping through her ears. The sound of her crying was the only noise in the room.

'You know, no one else has been brave enough to come up this mountain since Moira did a hundred years ago,' said Florence finally. 'Flint never made it this far.'

'I know. And look at the problems I've caused.'

Florence peered at her over the rims of her glasses.

231

'Ember,' she said, putting a wing to Ember's cheek. 'The world is full of problems; it always has been, and it always will be. But you know what the world *isn't* full of? People who try to make a difference.'

'But I *haven't* made a difference. I've failed.'

Florence laughed and shook her head. 'Thank goodness for failure. If we only ever did things we knew we could do perfectly the first time, well, that would be a rather boring life. Don't you think?'

Ember looked up. Her whole village lived that way – doing things they already knew they could do because the Fate Cards had said they would do them. But Hans and Florence didn't. They seemed to dive into everything, never worrying if they might be turned into a bookworm, or stuck in a nightmare land – not if it meant helping their friends.

'You know, this is my seventy-second time trying to start a newspaper,' Florence continued. 'But finally, I think I've got a front page worth reading – if we ever get out of here, that is. Part of the adventure *is* failing. Otherwise, it's not really an adventure at all.'

Ember swallowed back another bout of tears. 'It's just . . . it's hard picking yourself up again and again.

At some point, haven't you got to admit some things are impossible?'

Hans leant forward, his eyes wide and unusually serious. 'Your father, one of the most marvellous men in the world, saved your life. He broke the fate designed for him, all because he wanted to save you. Wasn't *that* impossible?'

'Yes, but—'

'But he did it. Not to mention, I'm a talking clock hand. Isn't *that* impossible? And climbing Mount Never and getting through the Know-It-Hall and facing your worst fears? Didn't they all feel unbelievably-never-in-a-million-trillion-years *impossible*?' He began jumping on the spot, each jump higher than the last as he continued. 'Impossible, *impossible*, IMPOSSIBLE!' he roared, with one final bounce.

Panting, he grinned his toothy smile. 'But you did all of them,' he said. 'And now, you're the *only* person in the world who can take on one last impossible thing. Don't tell me you're going to give up now?'

Hans was right. Ember had already done so many impossible things. They hadn't always worked out how she had planned, but she had made it to the top. Yes, they were stuck in a basement, but that didn't mean it was over.

Ember wiped her face, brushed off her knees, stood up, and took a deep breath. 'You're right, both of you. It is better to try and make a difference than do nothing at all. If I had never come up the mountain, then I would never have met either of you and my life would be as boring and unadventurous as everyone else's in the village.'

'And you wouldn't have me as a friend,' Hans said, winking.

'A friend? Don't you mean a bestest friend in the whole world?' She smiled back at him.

His face lit up and he leapt into the air, let out a whoop and looped around and around Ember.

'You mean it?' he said, once he had finally stopped.

'Absolutely. Along with Juniper and you too, Florence! I'm sorry I haven't always listened to you, Hans. I've been so scared that we might get it wrong. But maybe it doesn't matter how many times we get it wrong, as long as we don't give up until we get it right.'

'Then I guess I should tell you!' Hans squealed. 'I know what we have to do!'

24

Hans was jumping from one foot to the other, bursting at the seams with excitement.

'I'm the hand!' he said, fighting between a whisper and a scream. He leapt into the air and pushed himself against the wall, drew his arms into his sides and did his best clock hand impression.

'Hans, I already know you're a clock hand.'

'Not *a* hand – *the* hand!' he said. 'I'm *Moira's* missing clock hand!'

The image of the numberless clock with a single hand that had been hanging above the Fateweaver's desk flashed across Ember's mind.

'I didn't even realise until we got here,' said Hans. 'But it makes sense now – why there were no other spare parts around except for *me*! Do you remember I told you how I used to be a thing?'

'Yes, you used to be a thing, and then you soaked up some magic from the forest, and one day you woke up as a living creature?'

'Exactly-actly-doo! All those memories from when I was a thing are foggy as anything, but the moment I saw that clock, and that other hand . . .' He stared at Ember. 'Wasn't she beautiful?'

'Who?'

'The hand, the other piece of me!'

Ember couldn't help it then, a smile spread across her face. 'So why aren't you on the clock?'

'Moira came from the village, didn't she Florence?' Hans asked. Florence nodded and Hans continued. 'I guess she must have snapped me off her clock in the Forest of Time, taken her clock with her and left me behind. Remember what I said happens if you take one hand off a clock?'

Ember did. He had told her in the forest when they first met: that if she had simply taken one hand from Juniper's clock, it would have stopped her from ageing. If only Ember had listened to him back then.

'So Moira has been stuck at the same age for a hundred years? But if we put you back—'

'Then *tick, tock, tick, tock* and *kapow*!'

'Hans, you're amazing!'

'I know! Hans Christof Sanderson can take my name, but he can't take my brains!'

Ember picked him up and hugged him, twirling around. Then she stopped. They still had a problem. It didn't matter if Hans was the missing hand. They were trapped in this room, with no way to get him back to the clock.

Ember bit her lip and tucked her hair behind her ears. 'We need a plan to put Hans back. Florence, how's your wing?'

Florence shuffled her feathers and stretched out her hurt wing, wincing as she did.

'I don't think it's broken, just sprained.' She started to flap, gently at first and then harder, so a breeze formed around them. But her face was creased in pain and she let out a tiny hoot. 'It's no use. It's not strong enough.'

'Never mind,' said Ember. 'We'll figure something out.' Ember thought hard. She was an inventor. What was the first rule of inventing? Use what's around you.

She grabbed her bag and pulled out everything she had brought with her. There was the bookrest she had made for Juniper, the set of tools from her dad, the Nothing-Goes-Bump-In-The-Light, the Auto-Quill – missing its ink – and a packet of matches, along with some scraps of metal and screws.

The Nothing-Goes-Bump-In-The-Light was still glowing softly. She shook it again until it began to grow brighter, bit by bit. Then, she eyed the oil lamp in the corner. Like a wave of inspiration, the Fixer's Feeling washed over her. She just hoped this time it was enough. She picked up the lamp, blew it out, and began to take it apart.

She would have to work quickly. One hand on the base, she pulled a piece of wire away from the lamp. Then she gently removed the feather from her Auto-Quill. From her toolbox, Ember chose a flathead screwdriver and started to chisel away at the wall, as quietly as she could, until she could pull a long length of wood from it. She attached the wood to the quill with wire, making a T-shape. She removed another piece of copper wire from the lamp and then held up her invention.

Florence hopped forward without a word and spread her wing open wide. Behind her glasses, her eyes glinted in the brightness of Ember's lamp. They could do this. If they all worked together.

'OK, let's see if this works.' She held the piece of wood close to Florence's body and wrapped the wire around her wing and the wood to keep it snugly in place. The feather from the quill fit over where Florence's wing was bent. Hopefully, it would be enough to strengthen it.

Within seconds, Florence was gliding above them, wearing her new splint. She faltered a few times, but it was much better.

'Thank you, Ember. I knew you could do it.'

But Ember was already working on the next thing. She tore a piece of cloth from her backpack and dipped it in the oil from the lamp. Carefully, she tied the wick around a corner of it, bunching it together to create a good knot. Balancing it on top of Juniper's bookrest – she didn't want to burn the whole place down after all – she gingerly placed her invention directly under the trapdoor. Finally, she set the box of matches down next to it, leaving a single match on top.

Without saying anything, Florence stood in front of the contraption, casting a shadow to shield it from anyone above. Then, Ember tore two more strips off the backpack and handed them to Florence and Hans.

'Hold these over your nose and mouth, you'll need them to stop you from breathing it in.'

'Breathing what in?' asked Hans.

Ember crouched down and looked them both right in the eye. 'This is going to be dangerous. You need to listen very carefully.'

Florence and Hans listened while she explained the plan. When she was done, they took one look at each other, then back at her, and nodded.

Their team was ready.

25

The trapdoor lifted above them and light flooded the basement.

'Well,' came the voice from above. Moira leered over them. 'Have you decided?'

Ember's heart was really starting to thump now. This was it. The last chance for them to save Juniper and stop the Fateweaver.

'Yes,' she said. 'You haven't given me much choice. So, I'll do it.'

Moira said nothing. Her face was in shadow; Ember couldn't tell what she was thinking.

Ember swallowed. 'This way, I'll know my fate,' she continued. 'It's much safer to know what will happen in your life. Otherwise, I might fail over and over again.' Was she convincing Moira?

The tension pulsed around them. Everyone held their breath. Moira leant forward and the light fell across her. Her eyes were lit like candles in a pumpkin.

After a long pause, her face broke into a smile. 'I knew you would do it! You don't belong down there in Everspring, Ember, you never have. You're like me, you'll see.'

Then suddenly, Moira's head disappeared, letting the trapdoor slam shut behind her. Footsteps sounded above and soon after, she had returned with a rope ladder.

'It's time to show you what I do here.'

Ember grabbed her toolbox and looked back at Hans and Florence. With a deep breath, she started to climb. Moira reached down to help, and Ember tried not to shudder as she felt her cold, smooth hand clutch her own.

'How does it work?' Ember asked, pointing at the machine. If her plan was going to work, she needed to learn everything she possibly could about that machine – and fast.

Moira let the trapdoor close over Ember's friends and within a second she was back to the smiling tour guide they had met in the Messy Middle, clearly thrilled to have someone to speak to. 'It's quite powerful, really. And I built it all myself! But I must start at the beginning.' She straightened her blazer and stood up tall. 'Your village, Everspring. That was once *my* village. And it was awful. We had children starving, we had grown adults who couldn't read or write, all living without any purpose. No one wanted to become a doctor at one point, so there was no one to treat sick and injured citizens. By the time the village realised there was a problem, it was too late because no one had studied science or medicine. Without being given a purpose, no one had learnt the skills needed.' Moira paused for a second. 'My mother died because of it. There wasn't anyone to help her.'

Ember's stomach turned. Losing a parent was hard, she knew that better than anyone.

Moira ran her hand along the machine lovingly. 'I couldn't stay in that horribly chaotic place after that. I felt helpless, not knowing what terrible thing was going to happen next. So, like you, I decided to climb the mountain. I found my clock. That was the first thing I improved. It was wildly swinging between different ages, a new one every second, no sense of order! So I fixed it. But that wasn't the end.

'I thought the Messy Middle was the answer. If I could control everyone's middle, then there would be order and balance in the village. People would have to do the job I told them, and there would be harmony. So I built the train engine and tried to organise that awful rollercoaster. But it didn't work because the Threads of Fate were still running wild all over the mountain.'

'So you came to the top, where the threads begin.'

'Exactly. Just like you. See, we aren't so different!' Moira said, winking at Ember. 'Anyway, it didn't take me long to realise that controlling the threads was the answer.'

Ember hated the pride in Moira's voice. It reminded her of whenever *she* had invented something herself, the way she wanted to show it off. But she had never created anything this monstrous.

'So, how exactly does the machine work?' Ember asked, appealing to Moira's vanity.

'It's a mixture of things, you see. Firstly, the threads come out from the mountain directly into my machine. There, they wait for a fate. I decide when the child the thread is connected to is old enough to have their destiny assigned. Some of them are harder to catch than others, so those children get their cards a bit later.

'Then, the vice inside this funnel grabs a thread and holds it in place while the machine chooses a fate. When it's got one, it ties knots into the person's thread – those knots determine the important life events, who they marry, when they die, all those sentimental sorts of things. *Before* my machine, those knots were created when a person made a choice, or set their future in a new direction. Now, my machine does it all for them!'

Her teeth flashed in a smile before she continued. 'Then, the only direction the threads can go is out the funnel. The threads burrow into the walls – trying to escape, I suppose – but as long as their other end is still trapped in my machine, they can't go far. But they do struggle.

'Sadly, knotting fates into the threads and keeping them trapped *still* wasn't enough to keep people's will from changing. The threads kept trying to untangle their knots and change the person's destiny. So I created the cards.'

She tapped the window where the stack of cards lay, waiting for instructions.

'The cards cement it for people, make sure they don't stray from the path. Turns out people are only too happy to follow a fate laid out for them. It's safe. It's the unknown that's so scary. And anyway, *no one* believes they can change something as powerful as fate.'

Ember thought back to receiving her own blank card, and to Flint's fear of getting his. Moira was right; not knowing the future was terrifying . . . but it also meant anything could happen. And that had to be better than living life based on someone else's plans.

'What about when someone steps on the mountain? Does the machine wipe their fate away?'

Moira smirked back at her. 'That little tale was nothing more than a rumour I started to make sure no one ever followed me up here.' She clasped her hands together and beamed at Ember. 'Oh, you must be so happy! As my apprentice, you finally have a future. You have a fate. And I have *you*. Someone here, someone to talk to. Someone like *me*.'

A shudder ran through Ember's bones, but she tried to smile back at Moira. The idea that she was like the Fateweaver was too much to hold in her mind for even a second, so she pushed it aside and focused on the machine and the house.

'How do you know which fate to assign?' she asked, trying to hide her horror by sounding impressed. 'How does that work?'

'That *is* an interesting question. It was exhausting, trying to decide which fate to give each person. Would someone be better as a doctor, or a teacher, or should they be an artist? First I tried assigning different purposes to numbers, and hoped that if I randomly selected a number for each person, some sort of balance would prevail. But it was useless. Then I tried writing all the fates myself for a while, one by one. That's what the keyboard was for.'

She pointed to the second, older keyboard, with the buttons across the bottom that said *Input Name, Input All, Edit* and *Send*.

'But every time I fixed a thread in place and assigned the fate to the card,' Moira continued, 'the house would start tipping one way or the other. You see it reflects the world below, and down there, nothing was balanced, there was still so much chaos. So this button,' she tapped the one that said *Balance*, 'well, it's probably my greatest invention yet. It selects the exact fate needed to create perfect harmony. I don't have to decide a single one! It also meant I could expand my operations beyond Everspring. I now give cards to every single person whose thread comes from Mount Never. That's twelve villages, four towns and one city, all thanks to this invention right here.'

Ember ran her fingers over the *Balance* button. It didn't sound so bad when Moira said it like that. It made sense, sort of. Moira had wanted to make things better, like Ember had. In fact, Moira had sacrificed everything to make it better: her family, her home, her own future. She had been alone for a century, all because she wanted to make the world a better place.

But Ember couldn't shake the fury that tightened around her when she thought about the cost of it all, the people it had hurt. Children fated to die young, dreamers giving up their passions because of words on a card, sweethearts married off to someone who Moira's machine had decided was good for them, rather than who they loved. Her own mum had cast aside her dream of writing like an old cardigan. It just wasn't right.

All because of this button, and this woman.

They had put so much faith in those Fate Cards. But the cards weren't divine mountain magic. They were the makings of a selfish woman and a button.

'The lever here, that's what keeps the vice tight,' Moira carried on, pointing. 'But somehow, yours slipped through, and your father's. Probably something to do with all the strength of mind you both have.'

'The ink,' Ember said, a thought suddenly springing to her. 'How does the ink on the Fate Cards work?'

Smugness spread across Moira's bony face. 'It's mixed with water from the well outside to reflect a person's fate. Once a fate is set, and the knots are tied, the machine will write it out and it will remain on the card for ever. But if I decided to change the fate, well, the words would change.'

'You really are a very good inventor.' Ember meant it. But she knew there was a difference between a good inventor and an inventor who uses their ideas to do good.

'It takes one to know one!' Moira smiled. Her eyes were shining. 'And with you by my side, we can expand beyond Mount Never to fix all the fates of the world, even the difficult ones like yours, and we will be unstoppable. Together, we can make sure that everyone's fates are mapped out, for ever. We can—'

Suddenly, Moira's head snapped around, her eyes alert and her nose wrinkled up as she sniffed, twice.

Ember could smell it too.

Smoke.

26

The smoke came thick and fast. It seeped from the edges of the trapdoor and spread out into the room, infecting the air. Dark, black smoke.

'What have you done?' Moira shrieked, running over to the trapdoor.

Ember dropped her toolbox next to the machine and sprinted after her. She hoped Florence and Hans were ready.

It all happened so quickly. Moira opened the door and a cloud of smoke billowed out. For a second, Ember couldn't see anything, until wings started flapping around her face, clearing the smoke. She ducked to the floor where it was clearer. Ahead of her, the Fateweaver was staring into the trapdoor, panicking as she looked for the source of the fire.

Ember crawled forward, blinking to rid the smoke from her eyes, covering her mouth with her sleeve.

There was so much smoke, maybe too much. Had she ruined everything again?

Dragging herself along the floor, she stretched her arms out and pushed, as hard as she could, against the backs of Moira's bony calves. Moira's legs buckled and her arms flailed, until she fell, right into the open trapdoor.

'Florence, we need water!'

The sound of wings clapped above her and Florence swooped into view. In her beak, she held the bucket from the well that had sat next to the Fateweaver's desk. Diving past the opening in the floor, she dropped the bucket and all its contents right on top of Moira.

Slowly, the smoke cleared.

Ember's heart drummed into a frantic rhythm as she stood over the side of the trapdoor and stared down at the soaked, sooty, Moira. It wasn't over yet. The Fateweaver glared up at them and began to clap. 'Bravo, bravo, very clever,' she said. 'And what do you plan to do now? Did you forget that I've acquired some magical abilities since being on the mountain?'

'Quickly!' Ember shouted at Hans, as the *POP* filled her ears, just as she had expected.

She only hoped she had bought them enough time.

Moira reappeared instantly, inches from Ember's face, her back to Hans and Florence, her eyes filled with rage and wet hair clinging to her face.

'You think you can trick me? I'll cut your sister's thread into a thousand pieces!' she screamed.

'I don't think so,' said Ember. 'Don't you recognise my bestest friend in the whole world?' Ember looked over Moira's shoulder at Hans, who was hovering in mid-air, in front of the clock above the desk.

'That's me!' he chirped.

Moira gave him a stony glance. 'And why would I recognise . . . *that*?'

'Because Hans here is your missing clock hand.'

Any colour that had clung to Moira's face disappeared, leaving a shocked expression behind. 'No! My clock hand wasn't alive! It was just a hand. A bit of metal!'

'And look at me now!' said Hans, giving a twirl in the air to show how animated he had become. 'You're not the only one who has soaked up some of the mountain's magic.'

Moira took a step forward, her eyes darting. There

was no way she could *POP* fast enough to reach Hans, and it looked like she knew it.

'Hans,' Ember said. 'Are you sure about this? We don't know what will happen once you're up there.'

'It doesn't matter. I will have done everything I ever wanted to do! I've helped the great, wonderful, marvellous Ember Shadows.' He leant towards the clock. 'Tick, tock, time,' he whispered, and he swivelled in mid-air, ready to join his feet to the centre of the clock.

'Wait!' called Moira, and Hans stopped. 'Ember, don't you want to see your father's card?'

She snapped her fingers and, swarming to her call, a flurry of origami birds flew over Ember like sparrows. They zoomed towards Moira, where they regrouped to create a tornado of white before falling to the ground. Each one unfolded and Moira was surrounded by a ring of white cards.

Ember's heart thumped. She looked at Hans, then back to Moira.

'I can give it to you,' whispered Moira. 'I can show you what fate had in store for your father, everything he could have been, had he not died to save you.'

Ember watched as Moira clicked her fingers again and, from the pile around her, a single card floated into the air, all the way up to her outstretched hand.

Ember knew she had to keep her face still. She couldn't give away how much she had longed to see that card since the day it had disappeared from the family frame.

'You're the one who took his card?' She tried to hold her voice steady. Florence reached out a wing to her knee, but Ember brushed it aside.

'Of course I did. I had to take it the day he died, or people would see that fates *could* be changed. Without this card, people continue to believe in the mountain, in everything I've built, even more than they believe their own memories.' Moira was smiling again. 'It's right here. Everything you took from him – the life he could have lived.'

'But the words, they would have changed,' said Ember, her own voice barely more than a whisper. 'They would have changed when his fate changed.'

Moira's awful smile grew wider. 'Not this time. He put an end to his own future by saving you, and fate never even had the chance to write another path. The fate he *could* have had, it's here.'

It was so close. Everything Ember had wondered about her father's future. Everything their family could have been if she had been the one to die. It was all there, on a tiny white card.

But, for the first time ever, the pit in her stomach that had always opened up whenever she thought about what her dad might have been, didn't appear. It didn't even threaten to.

Because she knew that he had chosen her. He hadn't been destined to die. He'd made a choice, and he'd chosen her.

And she wasn't about to throw that away.

Ember looked over at Hans, then down at Florence. They were about to change Everspring for ever. They were about to put adventure back into everyone's lives.

'I'm sorry for what happened to you,' she said, holding Moira's gaze. Moira looked broken; a century of cheating death had taken its toll. 'But you have no right to live for ever, and no right to fix everyone's fates – nobody does. Life is supposed to be messy, and we aren't supposed to have it all mapped out for us. We can't control everything.' She paused, smiling at her new magical friends. 'We all need a bit of adventure in our lives – otherwise, what's the point?'

'No!' screamed Moira. 'You're wrong, you're all—'

'Hans, now!'

Moira's eyes widened in horror as Hans fixed himself to the clock on the wall with a long whoop. The second he did, he began to spin round and round the clock, the other hand spinning in the opposite direction. Ember's gaze flickered between him and Moira, who was now frozen with fear.

As Hans and the other clock hand turned, faster and faster, Moira's face began to crease with wrinkles. Her hair turned grey, her eyes sunk into her face and the bones in her back hunched into an arch. She was ageing, ageing in fast forward.

Her skin started to flake.

Ember looked away. She couldn't watch any more.

But Hans was slowing now. As he made his final tick, Ember turned back to Moira.

Nothing but a pile of ash, surrounded by hundreds of motionless white cards, remained.

27

Ember's heart seemed to come to a stop as the silence festered around them.

Together, she and Florence rushed over to where Hans hung on Moira's clock.

He was still fixed to the centre and was now pointing to the bottom, resting on top of the other hand as they both dangled, lifeless. His eyes were closed, and his hands were back in line with his body; his infectious toothy grin was gone, replaced with only a thin line.

Ember reached her hand out, scared to touch him and have her worst fears confirmed. As her fingers met his metal skin, she was surprised to find he was warm. A glimmer of hope started to blossom inside her. Could he still be alive?

'Hans?' she whispered. 'Can you hear me?' But the hope that had glowed like a firefly in her chest flickered and dimmed as she got no answer. 'Hans?'

He had gone.

All that was left of her friend was a piece of metal.

She turned back to face Florence, trying to swallow down the lump rising in her throat, when suddenly, a loud squeal filled her ears, and Hans rocketed past her head, looping, twisting and screaming with joy like a balloon letting out all its air.

'We did it!' he shouted, as he zoomed around the room. 'We did it!'

'Hans! You're alive!' Ember laughed with relief as he wrapped his tiny arms around her head.

'I am,' he said, sounding shocked. He pulled back from her and frowned, confusion etched all over his face. 'I thought once I had fulfilled my destiny . . .'

Through blurry tears, she beamed at her friend. 'I think that's the point about being alive, Hans. You can choose your own destiny, and once you've fulfilled that one, you don't stop living. You find a new one.'

He smiled back. 'Maybe you're right. And guess what – I wasn't a spare part after all!'

'Of course you weren't,' said Ember, clinging on to his hands as he hovered in mid-air. 'You never were, you've always been a *huge* part of this team.'

Hans blushed a deep, silvery shade of pink. 'You know, the people in your village are lucky to have the super, marvellous, wonderful Ember Shadows looking out for them.'

'It's not over yet,' she said. 'We still have to save Juniper and fix the mountain.'

She ran over to the machine, hoping that they weren't too late. They had no way of knowing how much time Juniper had left now, but she guessed it was minutes. With two hands clasped around the machine's lever, she pulled hard, and a thunderous creak erupted from the machine, announcing that the vice had opened.

Ember's eyes darted to the ceiling.

Nothing happened.

Why weren't the threads moving?

'Can you break the whole thing?' said Florence as she flapped around the threads above.

'Smash it!' screamed Hans, clearly fired up from his near-death experience.

The cards. Ember frantically tried to think. The Fateweaver had said it was a combination of the machine and the cards that held the villagers captive. Her mind whirred as the pieces fell into place – the Fate Cards weren't destiny. They were just a tool to convince everyone in Everspring that there was only one way to live life. As long as they were convinced by the cards, their fate wouldn't fight back against the future Moira's machine had chosen for them.

So if she wanted to change things, *really* change things, and allow people to carve their own paths, the people of the village had to know that they could choose their own destiny. Juniper and everyone else in the village had to know their fates were free. And there was one other thing she had to do, too.

'We still need to fix the broken wheel in Juniper's clock. Florence, can you get my bag from the basement?

And Hans, can you get a replacement wheel from the Fateweaver's clock?'

Florence nodded, Hans saluted her and the two of them got to work.

Ember focused on the machine's window where the cards lay motionless. Carefully, she examined the buttons below. She had to do exactly the right thing. Exactly.

'If I do this, the house is probably going to start tipping again, so we need to be ready.' Once Florence had retrieved her bag, Ember took out Juniper's clock and gave it to Hans, who was carefully extracting a wheel from Moira's. 'When you've got the piece, I'll need you to fix Juniper's clock. Hans, I'm trusting you to do this.'

He grinned back at her as he worked, his tiny fingers perfect for the job.

Now, she just had to change every single card in the village.

First, *Edit*.

Only a quiet *click* told her it had been registered. But as she went to press the next button, a tiny flicker of movement came into her vision. A thread, a golden one so fine it could have been a ray of light, had twitched. She was sure of it.

She pushed *Input All*. Another *click*.

Now she had to write.

She took a deep breath and looked at Hans, who gave her a thumbs up and tipped Juniper's clock face towards her. It was back in one piece, and the hands no longer hung limply at the bottom. Instead, they had returned back to the numbers zero and eight.

Her mouth dry, Ember's fingers hovered over the keys. For a second, her mind went horribly blank.

But after a quick glance at her toolbox, she knew exactly what to say.

She typed out a message.

Taking one last, deep breath, she hit send.

Ember looked up at the threads, each one exactly where it had been before, except hers, which was still flying around the ceiling.

'How do we know if it worked?' whispered Florence.

Juniper's card. Ember rummaged in her bag and pulled it out. There, in black ink, were Ember's own words.

It's time to write your own fate. Your only limit is your imagination.

It had worked. Once people saw their cards, they

would start to consider the endless possible directions their lives could take. They would start to dream a little more, free to make their own decisions. And, hopefully, their threads would start to move.

'Ember, look.'

A thread above Hans' head had jerked. It was thick and brown, almost a rope, and it had started wiggling free from the machine. Someone had seen their card. Someone had thought of the other possibilities.

'We did it!' she screamed. 'We actually did it!'

The three of them jumped and spun around, Florence flapping her wings and Hans doing a funny sort of jig. Above them, one by one, threads started to break free, pulling and shooting all over the room, loosening the knots Moira's machine had tied.

'Now let's get out of here before—'

The house started to sway, enough for Ember to feel like she was at sea. 'Quickly! Get to the door!'

Hans shot through the air, Florence took off with speed and grace, and Ember clambered as best she could to the exit, where they all tumbled down the steps and on to the ground.

But everyone was all right, and in a bundle of arms,

legs and wings, the three of them began to laugh.
Through the open doors, Ember watched as the threads
flew across the room like starlings.

One smashed its way right through the window,
zipping through the fresh air and into the forest beneath,
free at last. Then another came, and another, bashing
into the machine as they went, until suddenly, with one
enormous *smash* from a vine-like silvery thread, a loud

creaking noise broke through the air, and the machine was ripped from the floor.

Hundreds of small threads that had been trapped inside it, without a fate yet assigned, burst out in an explosion of colour. As the house swayed, the huge, ugly contraption began to slide across the floor and smash into the walls, skidding from one side to the other. Empty Fate Cards were crushed under its weight

267

and torn to pieces. Nuts, bolts, screws, dial hands, everything came crashing apart.

'Will it stop? The house, will it stop moving?' asked Hans.

'Maybe one day,' said Ember, brushing off her knees. 'But the next time it balances it will be because the world has kept balance itself. Not because some Fateweaver wants to control everyone.'

Hans held up Juniper's clock. 'Ember . . . it still hasn't moved.'

Of course. Juniper still believed she was going to die very soon and that belief was a powerful one. She needed to see the new message on her card as soon as possible.

Ember turned to Florence. 'I need you to take my sister's card to her as fast as you can. Do you think you can fly down the mountain for me?'

'It would be an honour,' Florence said, and opened her beak to carry the card.

'And Florence,' Ember said, as the owl spread her wings. 'Thank you. We couldn't have done this without you.'

'My dear, I've been in that garden for quite some time, too terrified of getting stuck in the Land of Fear to try and come to the top again. You've not only helped me face my fears, but you've also given me the best front page a reporter could ask for. I should be thanking *you*.'

Her eyes twinkled and she plunged through the clouds, right down the side of the mountain.

'Hans, we need to get down the mountain too!' said Ember. 'Do you think—'

'Help! Help! It's after me!'

An unmistakable voice screamed through the forest, along with a great roaring, thundering sound.

Flying up the path was Flint, riding what looked like some sort of motorised bike with skis attached. Chasing him was a huge, thick, black Thread of Fate.

'HELP ME!' he squealed. 'This thing's gonna kill me!'

He slammed on the brakes and skidded to a halt in front of Ember and Hans, tumbling off the bike. The thread took the opportunity to jump right on top of him, winding around Flint as he tried to wrestle it off.

'DON'T JUST STAND THERE. HELP!'

Ember fought her laughter and gently prised the thread from Flint. It lay motionless in her hand.

'Flint, I think this is your Thread of Fate!' she said.

'Can't be,' he said firmly. ' 'Aven't ever got a card, so I ain't got a fate.'

'Everyone has one. I think, because you never received your card, Moira kept your thread trapped in the machine this whole time. Like how you trapped yourself on the mountain.'

Flint frowned, the cogs turning in his head. '*Moira*? What machine? And how'd the thread get out?'

Ember's eyes locked with Hans' and they both smiled. 'It's a long story.' She stroked the thread in her hand and it wriggled slightly. 'The point is, you get to choose your own fate now, Flint. No more cards.'

'No more cards? So I can do whatever I want?'

'Exactly.'

Flint's face lit up. Ember couldn't even imagine all the things he was thinking. He'd been hiding away on the mountain for so long, terrified of what was to come. But as a smile started to play around his lips, his thread started to uncurl. A moment later it snapped out of Ember's hand, paused mid-air, and then sprinted off into the forest.

'Where's it gone?' asked Flint.

'That's the exciting part. We haven't got any idea!' laughed Ember.

Flint's thread was finally free, and his life wasn't limited any more. No one's would be.

'Wait a second, Flint, how did you get here? I thought you were too scared to come up the mountain?' said Ember.

Flint's face turned a bright shade of pink. 'I – well, I wanted to help. I did try to call out to you. Did try to stop you going in that scary Land of Fear place. But you wouldn't listen.'

It had been *Flint* shouting her name, and the spluttering sound had been his bike. She knew she hadn't imagined it.

'I thought that if *you* could come all the way up, you know, being a kid and all that, that I'd been a bit silly, staying put for so long.' He sighed. 'I thought maybe it was time I stopped listening to all them worries.'

'You made it through the Land of Fear? That's great, Flint!'

He turned a deeper red, and muttered something Ember couldn't quite hear, apart from the words 'map' and 'tunnels'.

'WE CAN'T HEAR YOU,' yelled Hans.

'All right, all right,' Flint said, looking at the ground. For some reason he seemed very reluctant to meet Ember's gaze. 'I didn't have to go through the Land of Fear. I've got a map of the mountain that shows a bunch of secret tunnels. I found it a long time ago in the Know-It-Hall, and well, no one else was going to use it, so I took it. It's easier to get through them than having to pass tests in all those realms, especially with my quad-sled.' He gestured sheepishly at his strange bike machine.

For a second, Ember thought she might explode. Flint had known how to get around the mountain all along and had been keeping it a secret!

But as she looked at him, her anger simmered down. Flint had only been eleven when he left the village. All this time, he had been alone. He had never been able to grow up properly. No wonder he'd been scared and unsure of whether to help her or not.

'Never mind, Flint,' she said. 'Maybe you can help us now. We need to find a way to get off this mountain and down to the village, fast.'

Flint looked even more uncomfortable than before. He took his hat from his head and began twisting it in his hands. His eyes darted to the carpet of cloud around them, and back to his bike. Ember frowned.

'What's wrong?'

'All this time, I thought if I went down then I'd have to follow a Fate Card. Guess I had a reason not to go back. But now . . .' He paused. 'What will my family say? My mum and dad?'

'They're your family, Flint. Believe me, they just want to have you back.'

'But what if they don't want me there? What if they're mad that I left? What if—'

'It's scary, isn't it?' said Ember. 'There are so many *what ifs* in the world, and suddenly we don't know the answer to any of them. But now, at least you have the chance to make your own decisions.'

'What if they're really happy to see you?' whispered Hans. 'Isn't that a *good* what if?'

Flint took a deep breath, as if trying to fill himself up with courage. Then he nodded. 'All right then. I'll come back!'

'We still have to find a way down,' said Ember.

'Well, that's easy,' said Flint, climbing aboard the quad-sled. 'Hop on!'

Hans' face was a picture of excitement.

'Can't we use your map to find a shortcut down?' Ember asked. The thought of racing down the mountain on that thing was not what she had in mind.

'The fastest way down is on the surface,' Flint said, pointing at the clouds below. 'I've waited twenty-five years to go home, no point waiting any longer.'

What other choice did she have? Anyway, she *had* survived a whole adventure – why not go on one more crazy journey? 'All right, then,' she said. 'I suppose we'd better get going.'

The engine roared into action and Hans let out a squeal as he and Ember climbed aboard, putting their fates into Flint's hands. And together they all hurtled down Mount Never.

28

Three Weeks Later...

On the banks of Border River, Ember dipped her feet into the water. The cold nibbled at her toes and ripples sloshed around her ankles. She'd forgotten how much she loved the feeling of water on her feet.

After weeks of winter threatening to take over from autumn, an unexpectedly warm day had snuck its way into Everspring. Ember knew the mild weather wouldn't last for long before the icy clutch of winter set in for good. So, with the sun beating down on them, she and Hans had decided to make the most of it by planning a picnic with Juniper and Florence.

Unfortunately, since trying food for the first time, Hans had become obsessed with very strange flavours, so there were jam and carrot sandwiches, jacket potatoes with blueberry sauce, and flasks of hot chocolate mixed with orange juice. Thankfully, Ember had made some snacks, too.

'It's really important that you stretch out your wing every day,' Juniper said now to Florence, who had been practising stretches on Juniper's knee. 'Not just when you come to visit.'

'Really, I don't have time for that, my dear,' Florence squawked. 'I have a newsroom to run nowadays, you know.'

Florence's newspaper had taken the mountain by storm. The different magical creatures loved hearing the news from other realms, and now it seemed everyone wanted to submit a piece to *Mount Never News*. Juniper had done such a great job fixing her wing that Florence was flying up and down the mountain most days, interviewing villagers and bookworms alike. Of course the statues in the Garden of Gifts had plenty to say, too.

'How are things down here?' said Florence.

'Some people are still worried without their cards,' explained Juniper. 'And that goes for the other villages who used to get cards, too. It's taking some getting used to. But mostly, it's getting better. People are starting to do what they *want* to do, not what they've been told. They're having adventures again.'

Ember pulled her feet from the water. It was strange thinking about how she had avoided the river all this time, and now she felt completely at ease sitting here next to it. But then, a lot had changed over the past few weeks.

Most importantly, Juniper had started recovering from her sickness almost as soon as Florence had delivered her card. She had decided to study veterinary science so she could help animals for the rest of her life. Or at least, until she decided she wanted to try something else.

'Have you decided whether you'll accept Ms Daylands's request, Ember?' said Florence.

The Council Leader, seeing how many villagers were struggling with the choices now facing them, had asked Ember to come and work for her. She said that she had been so impressed with the way she had inspired Flint to come home that she wanted Ember's help advising and inspiring all the people of Everspring to carve their own paths in life.

'I'm not sure yet, it seems like a big responsibility,' Ember said. 'Plus I need to keep working on my inventions. I've been helping Mum, though. She's started writing again and she seems happy for the first time in a long time.'

'Mum is the bestest mum in the world,' said Hans. He lay back with his hands behind his head.

Hans had pretty much become their brother now. He was sleeping in their house and eating more food than Ember ever thought possible. As for calling their mum 'Mum' – well, he couldn't understand why he would use any other name.

The sound of a spluttering engine broke Ember's thoughts.

Flint came skidding down the path towards the river and screamed to a halt in front of them.

'All right, everyone!' he said, as he swung off the quad-sled. 'How's it going?'

Everyone ran over to greet Flint, and Hans stuffed as many carrot and jam sandwiches into his friend's hands as he could.

'Got some big news,' Flint said. 'Moving day for me tomorrow! Wondered if you could all help?'

The day that they hurtled down the mountain, Flint had finally reunited with his family, after twenty-five years apart. There had been a huge celebration in the village and his parents were overjoyed. There were a lot of tears, fireworks and never-ending hugs of forgiveness. For years, Flint had been terrified of seeing his family again, thinking they would be angry at him for running away. But in the end, as Ember had known they would be, they were just relieved to have him home.

It was still difficult, of course. Despite all the excitement, Flint had spent so long on his own that it had taken him time to adjust to living back in the village again. Even for his parents, it had been hard – they had lost a child and now an adult had come back. So, to make things a bit easier, he had been splitting his time between his parents' house and his own home at the foot of Mount Never. That way, he said, they could get to know each other again without it being too overwhelming.

Tomorrow it seemed he would finally make the move back home properly, to catch up on the lost time with his family – not to mention all of his old friends.

Hans squealed. 'Moving day! Of course we can help, we are the best helpers Everspring has ever seen!'

Ember grinned. A few weeks ago, things had seemed beyond repair. She had no future, and a sister with only a few months left to live. But today, sitting by the edge of the river, she wondered if things could get any better. She had saved her sister, but on top of that, she had reunited Flint with his family, gained three wonderful new friends, and she now had her whole life ahead of her to keep making memories. Better yet, she didn't have to do it alone any more.

She turned and realised Hans had been watching her, his green eyes glinting in the sun. 'Thinking about how you've got the bestest friends in the world, Ember Shadows?' He nudged her in the ribs and gave her his widest toothy smile. 'Me, too.'

'By the way, Ember,' said Flint, standing up and reaching into the seat of his quad-sled. 'I've got something for you. Mind you, I don't think you should tell anyone you have it. And if I were you, I wouldn't be doing anything with it. In fact, I'm not even sure I should give it to you, but I thought best you have it after everything—'

'What is it, Flint?' Ember laughed, cutting off his rambling.

He breathed out, long and hard. 'Here,' he said, as he pulled a long brown tube from the bike and handed it to Ember.

She turned the tube over in her hands, feeling four pairs of eyes on her as she examined the strange shape. It was about as long as her arm, and made of a material similar to cardboard, but it felt older, and much more fragile. The end of the tube was made from the same thing, but was a screw-top, like the lid of a jar. She unscrewed it carefully. Something inside her started to flutter.

Ember reached her hand in and felt something thin.

Slowly, she pulled out a rolled-up piece of paper. Everyone seemed to hold their breath. Juniper leant forward as Ember put the tube to one side. Carefully, she spread the paper out between them, so all five of them could see it.

Hans let out a tiny gasp, and the butterflies in Ember's stomach zipped around, faster and faster, until she could hardly contain them at all.

There, drawn intricately on the paper, were *two* illustrations of Mount Never.

One of them was the mountain as Ember knew it, and the second was an image of the *inside* of the mountain, viewed as though it had been cut in half, right down the middle.

'It's the map,' whispered Hans.

He was right. It was the map that Flint had been using to get around the mountain, the one he had found years ago.

'But Flint, don't you think we should return this to the Know-It-Hall?' said Ember, trying to prise her eyes away from the paper. She was sure there would be some grumpy bookworms missing this special piece.

'What use is knowledge in a big maze, with no one there to use it?' Flint said. 'Nah, keep it, for now at least. Thought I ought to give it to you after everythin' you did for me, for everyone.'

She thanked him again and felt the buzz of excitement in her fingers as she traced the map's shapes. There, on the left, were all the realms of Mount Never, where the Threads of Fate now ran freely. There was the Forest of Time, illustrated with tiny clocks on trees, and the maze that made up the Know-It-Hall, then the Messy Middle, the Garden of Gifts, and the Land of Fear. Teetering on the top was the wooden building where the Threads of Fate emerged.

On the right side of the paper was the inside of the mountain. Her eyes widened as she scanned the picture – the mountain wasn't one big rock at all, it was hollow! Thin, black, snake-like shapes wove their way through the mountain, representing the secret tunnels that Flint had been using. But there was more, Ember realised, as she peered closer at the map.

Flint caught her gaze. 'Amazing, isn't it?' he said. 'The realms on the outside of the mountain are all there for the Threads of Fate. As people make decisions, the threads journey through them and it shapes what will happen in someone's life. But on the *inside* – well, the inside of the mountain actually *makes* the threads.'

Ember held her breath, overwhelmed by how much wonder was contained in the mountain. The whole rock was a magical factory, spinning threads, each one completely unique.

As she studied the map, something in the bottom right-hand corner caught her eye. A small, black, wax seal had been stamped on to the paper. Embossed in silver into the wax was the same symbol she had seen on Moira's pin badge: a jagged line surrounded by the four letters found on a compass. Close up, Ember realised the line appeared to be the outline of a mountain range, made of four peaks reaching into the sky. What was the symbol doing on this map? Beneath, the letters S.E.C.R.E.T had been hand-written in black ink.

She lifted her eyes to her sister, then to Hans, and then Florence. They didn't need to say anything. She could feel the excitement reverberating from each of them as Hans started to bounce in the air. The butterflies in her stomach zoomed around, looping and hurtling like the Messy Middle's train.

Just when she thought she had solved all of the mountain's mysteries, another seemed to have surfaced.

She looked up at Mount Never. For three weeks, not a single card had flown down from the top. It was still a bit strange, everyone making their own decisions, but things were working, and people were having adventures every day. Every sunrise brought with it excitement and the unknown. It was scary sometimes, not knowing what was ahead, but it was worth it, because they could choose their own futures.

As she stared at the mountain, her friends pored

over the map of the hidden world inside Mount Never, and the most thrilling feeling spread through her bones.

It was time for another adventure.

ACKNOWLEDGEMENTS

If at twelve years old, I had received a Fate Card saying one day I'd be a published author, I would never have believed it. And without this group of incredible people helping me every step of the way, it would never have happened.

Firstly, thanks to my unbelievable agent, Kate Shaw, who picked up Ember's story and believed in it from day one. To think how much this book has developed thanks to your enthusiasm, feedback and support, I'm eternally grateful to have such an incredible person in my corner. It wasn't long ago I was reading the acknowledgements of other authors who sang your praises and I'm so proud to be able to do the same now.

Thank you also to my fantastic editor, Lena McCauley, for having such a clear vision for Ember beyond what I could have ever dreamt. I feel incredibly lucky to be working with someone so talented, and endless thanks go to you for seeing something in Mount Never and turning this story into the very best book it could be.

To the whole team at Hachette Children's Group, thank you for working so hard to get this into the hands of readers. To publicist Lucy Clayton and marketer Beth McWilliams, to desk editor Ruth Girmatsion, copy editor Genevieve Herr, proof reader Lucy Rogers, and to Helen Hughes in production. And of course, an enormous thank you to designer Samuel Perrett and illustrator Raquel Ochoa who brought the characters and the whole book to life in a way I could have only dreamt of.

Thank you to all those who gave feedback along the way, including my brilliant MA tutors Catherine Wilcox and Alex Wheatle. An extra-special thank you to four talented writers who provided inspiration, feedback and encouragement from the very start: Heather, Kate, Natasha and Rachael. I can't wait to have a stack of all our books together on my shelf!

Thank you to my incredible friends dotted around the world: Lucy, Katherine, Steve, Miley, Andreas, Courtney and James. I never let you read a word, and yet for some reason you all believed in me anyway.

And of course, always, thank you to my enormous family and extended family: Kings, Jopes, Walkers and Mottrams. To Gran and Baz, for showing me what it means to be brave and the importance of choosing our own paths in life. To Sue, Roy and Jack, for your unwavering support through every Zoom call in the lead-up to this finally becoming real.

To my sister, Charlie, for being such a huge part of my love of reading growing up, thank you. You introduced me to some of my favourite books, and I hope to repay the favour by doing the same for Felicity. And to my brother, Matt, you were a constant presence during lockdown when I wrote this, and then always at the other end of the phone afterwards. Thank you for all your positivity, encouragement and creativity.

To my parents, thank you for feeding my reading obsession by taking me to the library, reading to me at night, letting me take all those books on holiday, and for the midnight trips to the bookshops in homemade fancy dress. Thank you to my Dad, for your unwavering belief, constant encouragement, and for finally letting the monkey on a unicycle idea go . . . it's technically in print now so *please* let it go! And to my Mum, an enormous thank you for being my number one cheerleader. Thank you for reading every single draft of everything I've ever written, still insisting you loved it the hundredth time, and for making me believe that maybe I really could do this.

And finally, to Luke. Without you, I might never have started writing fiction at all. There are a million things I could thank you for, but for now, thank you for supporting me to follow my dreams every day and for picking me back up whenever I thought I couldn't do it. Most of all, thank you for a life so filled with adventure, that I know I'll never run out of ideas.

REBECCA KING was born in Wolverhampton, but spent her childhood in a tiny village called Sound in Cheshire. She studied Journalism at the University of Portsmouth, and has worked as a reporter and a primary school teacher, including three years teaching in China. She now lives in Bratislava, Slovakia, with her partner and her Chinese rescue dog, Mushu.

You can find Rebecca on Twitter
@RKingWriter

Look out for the next adventure

EMBER SHADOWS

and the LOST DESERT of TIME

Coming Soon!